A

```
CW01432838
```

LAST COPY

EIGHTH STEP FOR
MEENA

By the same author

Bâpû Had Eight Sons, The Book Guild, 2000

I Had a Fight on My Hands, The Book Guild, 2003

August the Nineteenth, The Book Guild, 2004

EIGHTH STEP FOR MEENA

V P (Hemant) Kanitkar

Book Guild Publishing
Sussex, England

First published in Great Britain in 2006 by
The Book Guild Ltd
25 High Street
Lewes, East Sussex
BN7 2LU

Typesetting in Baskerville by
Keyboard Services, Luton, Bedfordshire

Printed in Great Britain by
Antony Rowe Ltd, Chippenham, Wiltshire

A catalogue record for this book is available from
The British Library

ISBN 1 85776 963 5

Author's Note

This work of fiction deals with Chitpavan Brahmin emigration from the Marathi-speaking districts of Bombay Presidency in western India to the UK and the USA in the 1950s. The references to the Maratha history are well documented. The descriptions of systematic and intentional vandalism through 'fire damage' to houses and small industries owned by Chitpavan and other Brahmins in cities, towns and villages in western India are based on real events that took place in February 1948. The shooting of Mahatma Gandhi by a Chitpavan Brahmin intellectual generated a 'fire-storm' which overwhelmed the Brahmin community and drove many of them westwards to escape the poison of anti-Brahmin atmosphere. They set sail for the land of hope, justice and fair play.

Sakhaa Saptapadee bhava

Take the seventh step for a life-long
friendship and companionship

– a Hindu wedding mantra

Introduction

Marriage is a gamble, it is often said. In order to reduce the odds against a successful marriage, Indians, not only Hindus but other religious communities as well, have followed the practice of arranging the marriages of their sons and daughters.

Hindus believe that marriages are made in Heaven. A future partner is revealed to a respectable marriage broker by the planets in horoscopes. The horoscopes of the prospective bride and groom are closely studied in order to determine the degree of compatibility. Without knowing the two persons, without any idea of their natures, hopes, aspirations and expectations, likes and dislikes, the marriage brokers often declare that the marriage will last and that there will be children.

If the parents of the parties concerned are satisfied and if both families are of equal educational, financial and social status, the union is sanctified by the family priests in the presence of the god Ganesha, the family deities and the sacred fire.

All members of the extended families of the bride and groom, along with many friends, witness the ceremony. Inner feelings are kept hidden. Freedom of choice goes up in smoke as ghee is poured into the sacred fire. Reason is drowned in the chanting of the mantras. It is hoped that love will blossom after the marriage.

Many such marriages last for fifty or more years where

the wife plays a secondary role and suffers in silence. Very rarely is there a mutually supportive partnership. Hindu young women born in Britain insist on exercising their right to a free choice. Some parents object to this Western concept of love before marriage and try to arrange their daughter's marriage. Conflict is the result, sometimes leading to tragedy.

Some young women are able to select their marriage partner with the full blessing of their enlightened parents. Meena chose Ramesh and her parents approved. Will the marriage last?

Acknowledgements

Particular thanks are due to Milind and Jayshree Joshi for preparing the typescript with meticulous care. I am grateful to the editorial staff for making the story reader-friendly, and other members of staff at The Book Guild for processing the material through the various stages of production. The front cover photograph of the 'Seven Steps' ritual was taken by the author in January 1990. The Nandi temple mentioned towards the end of step five is Ashok's link to his native village in western India. The back cover photo is by Mrs Vaishali Ponkshe, Borivli, Mumbai, India.

Step One

November 1947 was a joyous month for Jay and Lata. They were to be married at the end of that month. Both families had long settled in Pune (Poona) and through their family priests and the marriage broker had come to know each other in the previous six months or so. Lata's father had been given detailed information about Jay's parents, their extended family, their educational, financial and social status. The family priests of both parties had carefully examined the horoscopes of Jay and Lata and had declared that the couple would find a high degree of compatibility in their marriage.

Jay's father was told that there was no such thing as a hundred per cent compatibility, but Mars and Venus were placed in the houses which controlled occupation and good fortune respectively. If Jay were to marry Lata, he would find happiness, professional success and good fortune and Lata would support him in all his lawful undertakings. But... 'Oh!' Jay's father had said. 'But,' the priest continued, 'the couple would prosper and the union would be fruitful if they crossed the five oceans and went to England.'

Jay and his parents had discussed the idea of going to England, where Jay could use his knowledge gained at the art school and get a job as a draughtsman.

'Dada,' said Jay to his father, 'you have no objection to my going abroad, have you?'

'No, Jay. Your elder brother will be here to help me. If

the horoscope prediction is right, you are more likely to prosper if you cross the ocean. It will be quite hard to adjust to a different lifestyle, but I am sure you will succeed.'

'I can't imagine what life in England would be like,' responded Jay. 'For a start I shall have to practise speaking English. I hope Lata likes the idea of living abroad.'

Jay's father had recently been promoted to the post of head clerk in the city magistrate's office where he had worked all his adult life after passing the matriculation examination. Jay's mother came from a small town in Pune district where her family had a home and two large fields cultivated by a tenant farmer. Jay's parents belonged to the lower middle class section of Hindu society. Working as a clerk in some office was almost the traditional occupation for a vast majority of men in lower middle class families. Living within one's means was second nature to such families because being in debt was considered a more deadly sin than stealing or causing physical injury to another person. Jay had an elder brother and an elder sister, both of whom were already married. So, after Jay's marriage, his father's responsibility towards his children would be over. Even after spending for Jay's marriage the family would be able to spare enough money, to help Jay leave India and settle in England. That was why Jay and his father had discussed the idea with guarded optimism.

'I am sure Lata and her family would have no strong objections to going to England,' said Jay's father. 'We can persuade Lata by pointing out that the standard of living in England would be a little higher than she would enjoy in India.'

At twenty-five, Jay was healthy, fair-complexioned and of average height for an upper caste Hindu from western India. He had qualified as a draughtsman at the art school in Bombay. The family priest had planted the seed of adventure in Jay's mind and gradually Jay had formed an ambition of going to live and work in England. He had begun to find out more about the social and economic conditions he would find there. India had just gained her independence after nearly two hundred years of British rule. Normally Jay would have had good prospects of attractive employment in independent India, but the Brahmin would be at a disadvantage when the dominant Maratha caste wielded political power and kept the Brahmin back through a calculated anti-Brahmin social and economic policy.

Lata was twenty-one, fairly good-looking, had passed the matriculation examination and was not likely to pursue further education because her father was a poorly paid clerk from a lower middle class family. When the priest gave Lata's family the result of his horoscope analysis, Lata and her parents and two sisters accepted the possibility of Lata's having to leave India and settle in England, if she were to marry Jay. In the weeks that followed before the wedding plans had been settled, Lata enthusiastically considered going to England after her marriage.

Jay's parents informed Lata's parents that the horoscopes matched very well and could they all come to the viewing ceremony, where Jay and Lata could see each other, exchange a few words and express whether they like each other. Only then would it be possible for both the families to discuss the wedding plans.

In return, Jay's father then received a note from Lata's father to say that he and his wife would be coming for the viewing ceremony the following week with Lata and her two sisters. That was in the third or fourth week of October. 'Jay,' his father said, 'the young lady will be here with her parents and two sisters on 29th October.'

Jay smiled with anticipation. He would meet the young woman who would probably be his wife. He had seen

Lata's photograph but a black and white picture did not give an accurate idea of the woman's complexion. He wanted his wife to have a light skin colour. Indians have this innate wish to have a light skin, maybe because the fierce sunshine in India burns the skin to a wheat-brown colour. Some people have to live with a dark brown skin. A light skin is equated to beauty even if the woman had a round face and plain features.

As arranged, Lata and her two sisters arrived with their parents on 29th October to meet Jay and his family. Jay's father welcomed them all and asked them to come into the sitting room of their modest house in Pune. After crossing the small unpaved front courtyard, the visitors followed Jay's father into the sitting room, where they were introduced to Jay, his mother and his elder brother with his wife. 'My married daughter is not in Pune at the moment,' explained Jay's father.

When Lata was introduced to Jay, he was glad to see that Lata did have a light complexion and neat features. As Lata smiled, Jay noticed her well-aligned teeth and a dimple on her left cheek. Her deep brown eyes appeared to him as twin pools of joy. Jay's father said that the marriage broker priest's analysis of the two horoscopes was very encouraging. Lata's father agreed with a vigorous nodding of the head. He pointed out that he would not be able to give more than a token dowry since he had to arrange marriages of the two younger daughters as well. Jay's father reassured Lata's father that the dowry was the last thing they had in mind.

'Would you let your daughter follow Jay to England, if they were to get married?'

'We have no objections. Of course after the marriage Lata will have to follow the wishes of her new family. I have discussed this question with Lata and she is willing to live abroad if Jay decides to go to England.'

'I am rather anxious,' said Jay, 'to settle overseas, because that is where I am likely to find success in my work, according to the marriage broker priest.'

Lata's parents were happy to note that Jay had a spirit of adventure in him and felt that he would make Lata happy. 'Lata,' said Jay, 'would you go to England and settle there?'

'Yes,' replied Lata.

'Are you sure?' asked Jay.

'Yes, I am sure,' responded Lata.

This frank exchange of intent pleased both families. It was mutually agreed that the marriage would take place in Pune as soon as possible and they would share the expenses. There was an auspicious day for the wedding the next month, and the booking of the hall would pose no difficulty. Jay's father also suggested that perhaps Lata's father would find about one thousand rupees necessary for Lata's clothes and travel expenses in about eighteen months' time. Lata's father heartily agreed to the suggestion, which was, he thought, cheaper than a dowry. Both families began the wedding preparations the next day.

Traditionally, a Hindu wedding takes place in the bride's home or in a hall hired by the bride's father. Lata's father, Appa, as he was affectionately known, went to see the manager of the Brahmin Marriage Hall in the centre of Pune and discussed the matter with him. The manager told Appa that the hall was free on 28th November and if Appa wished to book it, he would have to pay 25 rupees in advance. 'Of course we shall deduct that sum from the final bill.'

'What sort of facilities do you provide?'

'Well, our daily charge for the hall is 51 rupees, which includes cooking and eating utensils, floor coverings, storage drums for water and the two hundred or so wooden boards which will be needed in the dining hall.'

'We shall need the hall for three days – the 27th, 28th and 29th November. The actual wedding ceremony will be on the 28th, but we shall need the two days on either side of that date for preparation and clearing up.'

'Good, Apparao. I'll write down the dates as definite booking. Do you have any particular persons to do the cooking and serving the food and for the clearing up afterwards?' the manager enquired.

'No, we don't. Could you recommend some good workers for those tasks?' asked Appa.

'Yes – I shall engage two persons for cooking, three persons for serving the food to the guests and four workers for clearing up afterwards.'

'How much would they cost?'

'Normally the cooks get 30 rupees each for three days' work. The three servers will be needed only for one day; they will cost 30 rupees altogether for the three persons, and four helpers will be at your service for three days at 15 rupees per head. All these persons will have to be given food and they have two separate rooms where whey will sleep. Of course, the cooks and servers are Brahmins and the helpers will also be Brahmins.'

'Now let me see, the hall will be 153 rupees, the cooks will cost 60 rupees, the servers 30 rupees and the helpers 60 rupees. That comes to 303 rupees altogether.'

'Yes, that's right,' agreed the manager.

'Would you ask the cooks to came to our house so that both families can discuss the number of guests, the menu – especially the main sweet dish – and the shop where we can get all the groceries.'

The manager agreed to arrange the meeting between Appa and the cooks. He was given the addresses of both families. Appa paid 25 rupees deposit and went from the Brahmin Marriage Hall to see Jay's father and give him the details of the arrangements. When Appa walked through the front door, Jay's father got up from the floor covering and walked down three steps into the front courtyard to greet him. As both men came up to the sitting room, Lata's father said, 'I am known as Appa.'

'And I am called Dada,' responded Jay's father.

Jay's mother Tai came up to the door leading into the sitting room from the inner part of the house. Appa made his *namaskar* to the lady of the house by joining his palms before him in greeting. Then Dada gently hinted to Tai that a cup of tea would be much appreciated by the guest.

While the men waited for tea, Appa looked carefully at the sitting room and noticed that there was a thin cotton pallet with a white covering spread on the long cotton floor covering., with two cushions leaning against the wall. The three walls were painted with yellow emulsion paint and there were many pegs set in the walls for hanging clothes. On the fourth side of the room there was wooden latticework, with a latticed door in the centre opening out on to the front courtyard. This gave much light and ventilation to the room. There was also an electric light suspended from the ceiling in the centre, with a white translucent glass shade.

Appa was admiring the smooth teak door leading into the inner part of the house when Jay's mother came into the sitting room with two cups. Dada and Appa took the cups with smiles of appreciation. While they refreshed themselves with hot, sweet tea, Appa told of his conversation with the manager of the Brahmin Marriage Hall. Dada and Tai were happy to get the details, which they approved.

'When the cooks come to discuss the menu, I shall bring Lata's mother with me,' added Appa.

'A very good idea, Apparao,' said Dada. 'I shall make sure that Jay and his elder brother are present for the meeting.'

Taking leave of Dada and Tai, Appa hurried to his

home, which was about a mile away in a good Brahmin locality. Mai, Appa's wife, came out of the kitchen and with a smile told her husband that the midday meal was ready. Appa had a wash and went into the kitchen/dining area, where his two younger daughters had already taken their places on the seating boards on the floor. Lata, the eldest daughter, was beginning to serve salt, lemon and chutney on the four thalis. Mai usually served her husband and daughters first, and after their meal was over, she would sit on the seating board for her meal while Lata served her and kept her company.

Appa gave a full account of his conversations with the manager of the Brahmin Marriage Hall and with Dada and Tai, Jay's parents, to Mai and Lata. Mai suggested that they would have to buy many saris and blouse pieces for their daughters and for Jay's mother, sister and sister-in-law. Appa agreed and further suggested that shirts for Dada and his elder son would be suitable gifts, and perhaps they could consult Jay and have a lighter woollen suit tailored for him.

'Appa,' said Lata, 'I think you should get a shirt, cotton jacket and cream-coloured folding cap for yourself.' Mai seconded Lata's suggestion. Appa then wrote down a list of the items to be purchased in preparation for the wedding. He felt that a necklace of cultured pearls and four bangles would be a suitable gift for Lata. He did not want to spend too much for this marriage since he would need to use his savings for the younger daughters' marriages in the future. Appa then suggested that the walls of the sitting room of their house should be painted. Mai and Lata said that plain white emulsion with three-inch-wide red border all around would look nice. Appa agreed and said that perhaps the electric lights could do with new shades, probably bluish and made of translucent glass.

That afternoon Appa contacted the local painter and

decorator and ordered the emulsion paint and the lampshades. 'We could do the painting for 10 rupees extra,' said the man in the shop. Appa, without any hesitation, added 10 rupees to the cost of paint and lampshades and arranged for the painting to be done three days later. Thus progressed the preparation for Lata's marriage.

The very next morning Appa received a note from Dada to say that the cooks had been asked to come to Dada's house after four that afternoon, and would Appa and Mai come for the meeting. Appa answered the note saying that they both would be there.

Appa and Mai were greeted by Jay's elder brother at the front door and led towards the sitting room, where Dada and Tai with Jay were waiting. Soon the cooks arrived and introduced themselves, saying that Keshav was the head cook and Bal was the assistant.

'Dadasahib, how many guests will there be for the wedding feast?' asked Keshav.

'Well,' responded Dada, 'there will be 65 persons altogether from the bridegroom's side.'

'And 45 persons from the bride's side,' said Appa. 'That will make 110 persons altogether.'

'Apparao, we shall add another 20 to that number and cater for maximum 130 people,' said Bal.

When the final number was approved by both the families, Keshav explained that he and Bal prepared most of the wedding feasts that take place at the Brahmin Marriage Hall and they also did the shopping for the groceries with the help of the general servants. 'Now, can you tell me what main sweet dish you have in mind?'

Appa suggested that perhaps there should be some spiced rice followed by jilebees.

'Apparao,' said Dada, 'we think that the main sweet dish should be bundi or motichur ladoos instead of jilebees.'

'Both items would cost almost the same,' said Keshav.

'That settles it, then, Apparao,' said Dada. 'We shall have spiced rice and motichur ladoos.'

'Dadasaheb,' said Bal, 'do you want the usual sweet and savoury snacks such as shev, Pune mixture, and sakar pare fries?'

'Yes certainly,' said Mai and Tai at the same time.

'What vegetables shall we buy?' asked Keshav.

'Potatoes, aubergines and carrots for vegetable curry and green chillies and cucumber for relishes,' said Tai.

Keshav and Bal made notes about the conversation, listed the items to be cooked and the vegetables to be obtained from the market. He added banana leaves, tea, sugar, milk, betel leaves and the ingredients for making paan after the meal to the shopping list. Then they worked out the quantities of rice, semolina, sugar, ghee and the three main vegetables.

'Keshav, do the shopping at Sathe general stores and ask them to send the bill to me,' said Dada.

The women went into the kitchen to make tea for everyone while the cooks finally worked out the quantities for various items.

After they all had tea, Appa said that he was going to see the musician who provided the marriage band for the post-wedding procession of the couple from the hall to the bridegroom's house.

'Very good, Apparao,' said Dada. 'In that case, I shall arrange for the open-top car for the procession and also about eight petromax lights for that evening.' Jay and his elder brother listened very carefully to all that was said and agreed upon. There was no need for them to make any suggestions since Appa and Dada had covered all the points. The cooks left a few minutes before Appa and Mai. Almost eighty per cent of the preparations were now in hand. Time marched steadily towards the last week of November.

* * *

One evening in the second week of November, Jay and his elder brother Vijay went for a stroll up to the Parvati Temple complex on the hill, which had shrines dedicated to the god Shiva as well as to the god Vishnu. This temple complex was constructed during the rule of the Peshwas in the early eighteenth century; they were the first ministers of the Maratha Kings of Satara.

As the brothers climbed over a hundred wide steps to the top, Vijay began talking about Jay's job and the possibility of his going to live and work abroad. 'Jay, your present job is permanent, is it not?'

'Yes, but there is no future in it, both from the point of promotion and also the salary.'

'That is the story in all office or teaching jobs at present,' commented Vijay.

'The horoscope prediction is tempting. I am going to give it my serious consideration...'

'Don't be discouraged if you find the going a little tough,' said Vijay. 'Firstly, Britain will be facing hard times so soon after the devastating war in Europe. The country will be going through a slow process of rebuilding after the war damage. Secondly, most of the jobs will be given to the British. So it might be wise to wait for eighteen months before you make any serious preparations. At the moment the exchange rate is 13 rupees to the pound. So, start saving from next month.'

'How much money would I need to go to England, do you think?' asked Jay.

'The economy class passage on a ship will be about 60 pounds. You will need another 40 pounds or so for shoes, clothes, suitcase and a raincoat.'

'That is a 100 pounds or 1,300 rupees. I can save that much in two years.'

'You will need another hundred pounds as insurance until you get a job. Dada and I will be able to give you substantial help in two years' time.'

Jay was pleased to get that assurance from Vijay, and after viewing the images in the Shiva and Vishnu temple, the brothers climbed down the wide steps and walked back to their house.

The character of Pune, or Poona, as it was called during the British Raj, was quite different because of a large British presence in the city. As the British East India Company defeated the different constituent members of the Maratha Confederacy one by one, the British control of the Subcontinent gradually widened. The British rulers created 'cantonments' in major places where Indian resistance to foreign rule was strong. In such towns and cities there was a marked division between the residential areas for the British Indian Army with European officers and Indian soldiers and those for the Indian civilian population. These were distinct 'pink town' and the 'brown town' areas. If the different members of the Maratha Confederacy had presented a united front, it is quite possible that the Marathas would have been able to offer a successful opposition to the designs of the merchant company. But the five main props of the Maratha Confederacy, namely Gaikwar, Pawar, Sindhia, Holker and the Peshwa, instead of facing the 'enemy' together, looked in five different directions, thus declaring their lack of unity to the British, who devised methods to separate them and ultimately defeat them. The four northern props survived as vassal states, while the Peshwaship was abolished in 1818. The establishment of the cantonments in the vassal states continued even after the 1857 uprising, and this policy firmly established the British Raj for about two hundred years until 1947. The Raj was firmly based on military force, European 'superiority'

12

policy and the co-operation of the educated Indians.

Immediately after Indian Independence in August 1947, the 'camp' areas were populated by rich Indians and Army officers who lived in the detached houses with a lot of open space around them. The civilians, mostly middle class Hindus, lived in terraces or semi-detached houses with very little open space around them. These areas felt congested, with little room for improvement. The bicycle and the tonga – a one-horse vehicle – were the main forms of public transport, along with the corporation buses.

As Vijay and Jay walked towards their house they passed the tonga stand outside the college, where a strong horsey smell invaded their nostrils, and had to be careful to avoid being bumped by the cyclists as they crossed the main road.

Three days before the main wedding ceremony Jay's family and Lata's family performed the pre-wedding worship of nine heavenly bodies, in their respective homes. This ceremony of propitiating the nine planets is widely performed in many Hindu families in India, even in the first decade of the twenty-first century. Strictly following the texts concerning the home-based religious rituals, this propitiation worship of the nine planets should be done the day after the wedding ceremony but not all Hindu families observe the strict rule, and perform this *puja* – worship – at a convenient time, on either side of the main wedding ceremony. This private ritual was the start of the marriage celebrations for both families. Jay as well as Lata now felt committed to fully participate in the wedding ceremony which would change their lifestyles and bring additional responsibilities and duties to them as married householders.

On 27th November Lata, her two sisters, Appa and Mai got ready after an early morning bathing. The four servants were asked to come to the house with two handcarts, so that various items could be transported to the Brahmin Marriage Hall. The previous day Appa and Mai had opened their steel trunk, which they used as a safe to store their valuables, and taken out two silver pots, six silver beakers and six silver thalis. Mai and Lata washed them, dried them and put them in a large basket to be taken to the hall. These solid silver dinner utensils were to be used for the special groups, namely the bridegroom and his parents and the bride and her parents. Mai also took out from the trunk three silver trays for the *puja* materials, and the special utensils for the 'heavy scent', attar and rose water, which were used for welcoming guests. Lata had collected the heavy, gold-embroidered silk shawls and her specially purchased wedding saris with matching blouses. Mai and her two younger daughters also made sure that their ceremonial saris were put with Lata's saris, to be taken to the hall.

When the servants came to their house, most things were ready. The silver items and the saris were put in the metal suitcase for safety. There were baskets containing various items of grocery, small tins of ghee, betel leaves and ingredients for making paan, large bundles of banana leaves, coconuts, many copper utensils needed for the religious rituals, items of embroidery done by Lata to indicate her artistic accomplishments, mango leaves, ball of string and many other things, which might be needed at the hall. The servants loaded all these items on the two handcarts and covered them with a cloth before securing them with strong strings. Appa walked with the first cart and the women followed the second cart, to hall, which was almost twenty minutes away. After unloading the carts, Appa and two servants went back to the house

14

to bring light bedding for the five of them, because it would be necessary for them to stay overnight at the hall.

The cooks soon arrived and prepared a light lunch for everyone. In the afternoon, four of Appa's friends arrived to prepare the wedding plinth in the courtyard, by fixing four small banana plants at the four corners, arranging the seating boards for the bride, the bridegroom and the priests and preparing the sacred fire vessel with small pieces of wood, darbha grass and the sacred wood for the *homa*. Other items, such as ghee, large brass oil lamps, flowers, *puja* materials and garlands for the young couple, were to be got ready after midnight, so that everything would be ready for the early morning auspicious moments when the wedding would be performed. While the wedding ceremony square plinth was being got ready, the two cooks were busy preparing the savoury fries made with chickpea-flour and spices, roasted rice and peanut mixture and the sweet and savoury paras to provide snacks for everyone before the evening meal. Some distant relations and friends were expected to arrive from the nearby towns of Wai, Bhor, Satara and Talegaon and were going to stay overnight at the marriage hall. As Appa was conferring with the cooks about the numbers for the simple evening meal that day, and the main sweet for the main wedding feast dinner the next day, some of the guests arrived. They were welcomed by Appa and Mai before given tea and snacks along with the rest of the people, including the four servants.

The temporary sleeping area was the main dining hall. The seating boards were stacked in one corner and a large cotton floor covering was spread on the floor. This area was for the men and the boys. The women were to use the two small rooms adjacent to the dining hall. Fresh flowers were bought after the evening meal and two visiting women guests started to prepare the wedding garlands.

All the *puja* materials and the utensils were arranged on the wedding plinth. By midnight, everything was ready. Appa and his two close friends checked everything and, making sure that everyone was in the appropriate sleeping area, closed the front door of the marriage hall.

'Tomorrow is going to be rather hectic,' said Appa to himself as he lay down on the thin cotton pallet for a few hours' rest.

Appa awoke at four in the morning and immediately got out of bed. He folded the sheets and bedspread and spread them on the pallet, then rolled up the entire bedding and pushed it against the wall. He looked into the rooms next to the kitchen and noticed that the cooks and the four servants were up and about. He asked the cooks to make a large quantity of tea so that all twenty persons could be refreshed after their ablutions and bathing. There were four toilets, so there were no queues. There was a slight chill in the air and the cooks were able to provide hot water for bathing to those who wanted it. By seven in the morning everyone had bathed and drunk a hot cup of tea, the cooks had started to fry the semolina globules to prepare the laddoos. After that the vegetable curries would be prepared, leaving the rice till later. Appa, Mai and Lata had put on their ceremonial clothes.

The priests of both families arrived and announced that the auspicious time for the verses of blessings was two minutes after nine o'clock. Then they set up the altar for Ganesha and the Mother Goddess and got the materials sorted. By eight o'clock the Ganesha *puja* was over.

Jay, his parents and others in the family arrived and were welcomed with the traditional sprinkling of rose water. Mai also waved a ghee lamp in front of Jay to ward off evil influences, after applying a dab of red kumkum to his forehead. The bridegroom's party was taken to the reception hall, which would later be used as a dining hall. Lata was busy offering quiet prayers to Parvati and Shiva for a long married life and children. Many guests had arrived. Some were taken to the reception hall, others waited near the wedding plinth. Lata's maternal uncle had arrived the night before. He would bring Lata to the wedding plinth as soon as the priests requested the presence of the bride and bridegroom.

By a quarter to nine the guests had been given rice grains tinged with red kumkum to shower the couple with. Jay was called to come to the plinth and stand on one of the seating boards, holding a garland in his hands. A girl was holding a *kalasha* – a copper pot with some water in it and a coconut and mango leaves on top – as she stood behind Jay. The two priests held a shawl to form a screen in front of him. Then they asked for the bride to be brought to the plinth. Lata's maternal uncle escorted her and as soon as she stood on the other side of the screen, with another girl behind her holding the *kalasha*, the priests began to chant the verses of blessings. The first verse was complete just after nine. The guests gave their blessings in the form of rice grains as soon as the refrain was sung – '*Shubha Mangala Saavadhaan.*' The timing was perfect. Lata and Jay, on either side of the screen, received the blessings and felt the rice grains on their head at the precise auspicious moment of two minutes after nine. By the time the eighth verse was sung, the guests had begun to chatter. The priests folded the shawl screen, Jay and Lata garlanded each other and the girls with the *kalasha* applied the water in the pot to the eyes of the newly-weds, using a flower.

Singing the eight verses of blessings has been the traditional beginning of the Hindu wedding ceremony for many centuries. It probably became the established practice when child marriage was common in Hindu society.

17

Although the bridegroom and the bride were mere children – perhaps ten and six, or twelve and eight respectively – they did not cohabit until the bride had begun to have periods. By the 1940s the ages of bridegroom and bride were about twenty-two and sixteen respectively. Yet the ritual sequence in the ceremony had not changed.

After the first ritual of blessings, the bridegroom was formally welcomed with a little mixture of honey and yoghurt. It was at this ceremony, usually, that the dowry payment was made. If there was no dowry to be given, then the bridegroom was given other suitable gifts. Jay received a made to measure light woollen suit, a shawl and 11 rupees cash. Lata was given gold bangles and a necklace of pearls at this point.

The daughter was formally given in marriage. Lata's father, Appa, spoke the mantra after his family priest, which mentioned three paternal ancestors of the couple by name. Mai poured a spoonful of cold water after each word on Appa's cupped hands, which were above Jay's cupped hands, which were in turn above Lata's cupped hands. As the water trickled through these hands, it was collected in a copper dish by Jay's mother. After each complete utterance of the mantra, Jay touched Lata's right shoulder with his right hand to indicate his acceptance of the daughter in marriage. The daughter was given in marriage by Lata's parents and was accepted by Jay and his parents.

Lata and Jay stood facing each other after the parents had withdrawn. She asked Jay to promise her that he would be moderate in the performance of his *dharma* – social/religious duty – his *artha* – the earning of a living through lawful means and effort – and his *kama* – the enjoyment of the good things in life. Jay gave the promise of moderation three times, which pleased Lata, her parents and those guests who were standing near the wedding plinth.

Lata expressed three wishes: that she be blessed with good fortune, prosperity and children, and Jay put a few grains of rice on her head and said that he would support her in attaining those wishes. Then he expressed his wishes: to be able to perform his religious rituals well, perform his *dharma* and achieve success in his employment. Lata now put a few grains of rice on Jay's head and said that she would support him in fulfilling those wishes.

In describing the above ritual I have given the impression that the bride and bridegroom spoke the mantes. But that was not the case. The priests spoke the mantras and the couple performed the appropriate actions. This is normal in Hindu weddings in India. The mantras are in Sanskrit and many couples do not fully understand the meaning of the mantras. The priests do not bother to explain the meaning of the mantras, but most people present as guests do know the sequence of rituals and the actions involved in each. In the ritual where Lata was given in marriage, her father did say the words and later Jay actually spoke the promise of moderation in *dharma*, *artha* and *kama*.

While sitting on seating boards on the floor and facing each other, Lata tied a turmeric root with a soft cotton thread to Jay's right wrist and Jay did the same to Lata's left wrist, then Lata received her marriage necklace of black beads from Jay and his mother. In some families the bridegroom's mother is involved in this marriage necklace ritual.

Jay was asked by the bride's family priest to take Lata's right hand in his right hand while the priest chanted the mantra to indicate that the bridegroom had accepted the bride as his life-partner.

The marriage *Homa* is an important fire worship ritual

in which Agni, the God of Fire, is given oblations of darbha grass, short pieces of twigs taken from the Indian fig trees, banyan, pipple and udumber, from mango tree and from palasha shrub, grains of rice and wheat, and ghee. The bride's family priest says the mantra for each offering. At the end of the phrase the bridegroom makes the appropriate oblation, at which moment, the bride, sitting on his right hand, touches his right hand with her right hand to indicate her participation in the proceedings.

During this ritual, a lot of smoke arose up from the 'fire vessel' and made the couple's eyes smart and water. Some ghee was spooned into the fire, which activated flames and the smoke disappeared.

The next ritual, called 'roasted rice' *homa*, had three distinct stages. Jay and Lata, standing close to each other with their cupped hands touching and holding the roasted rice and ghee oblation, made the first offering to Agni, as the priest chanted the mantra.

Jay held Lata's right hand and asked her to follow him to walk round the fire together. The priest chanted the second stage mantra, which informed the guests that the couples wished to marry and have children.

For the third stage, Jay indicated to Lata that she should put her right foot on a stone slab and be firm as a rock, to defend her and her new family's honour. The priest chanted the mantra which coincided with the couple's action. This ritual was done twice more, the oblations being given to Aryaman, a Vedic deity and to Varuna, the Indian Neptune. The circumambulation of the fire and the stepping on the stone slab rituals were done in the same way as the first time. In the middle of this 'roasted rice' *homa* ritual, a distant cousin of Lata's stepped forward and pretended to twist Jay's ear, reminding Jay that he was now duty bound to take care of Lata in every way. Jay gave the 'ear-twister' a ceremonial flat cap as a token gift.

Jay and Lata then offered prayers to Agni, God of Fire, and asked for many blessings, and the priest sprinkled the couple with water from a cup which had a gold ring put in it. The sprinkling was done with a flower dipped in water to accompany the long mantra. Lata's parents then brought the ceremony to a close by offering thanks to the god for a trouble-free event.

There was only one more ritual left. The bride's family priest made seven small heaps of rice on the floor. Jay and Lata stood next to each other, with Jay's right hand on Lata's right shoulder. The priest asked them to walk seven steps together, taking each step with the right foot and bringing the left foot forward to stand still. The first step was for 'abundance of food', the second was for 'strength', the third for 'wealth', the fourth for 'happiness', the fifth for 'children, hopefully sons as well as daughters', the sixth step was for 'seasonal pleasures' together, and the seventh step was for 'life-long friendship and companion-ship'. After the seventh step ritual, the marriage was complete and binding. 'Lata's father, Appa, spoke his blessings to Lata and Jay, and the priest chanted his blessings for the couple and the assembled guests.

It was nearly eleven in the morning. Appa and Dada said a few words to each guest and thanked them for their presence. The cooks were busy cooking the main feast lunch and had prepared tea for those who wanted it. Many guests preferred to sample the savoury snacks. Jay and Lata, now husband and wife, after refreshments, took their places on the seating boards on the plinth. One senior member of each visiting family now came forward and gave items of clothing to Jay and Lata. Their parents made the 'return' gifts to each visiting family by giving them similar items of clothing. After this formal exchange of gifts, the guests were asked to take their places for the feast lunch in the dining hall.

Seating boards were placed in rows, with clean banana leaves in front of each board. All the members of the two families, the cooks and the servants were to have their meal at the second sitting. Appa and Dada supervised while the three Brahmin helpers served the food. The guests enjoyed the delicately spiced vegetables and lentils with rice and were given two or three helpings of the laddoos. After lunch, the guests were given betel paan as a mouth freshener and digestive aid. By four in the afternoon, everyone had had their meal and all the guests had left, and everyone rested for about three hours.

The band of musicians, the petromax light bearers and the open-top car arrived at the marriage hall when the night had begun her influence after sunset. When Jay and Lata were seated on the rear seat in the car, the post-wedding procession began to inch forward to Jay's house, which would be Lata's new family home. As the procession reached its destination, Jay and Lata left the car and stood outside the front door. A few spoonfuls of warm water and milk were poured on their feet, a dab of kum-kum was applied to their forehead and a ghee lamp on a tray was waved in a vertical circle in front of the couple to ward off evil influences.

A metal pot containing rice grains was put on the threshold and Lata was then asked to topple the pot gently with her right foot so that the grains spilled out into the house. This ritual implies that the new bride will bring good fortune and abundant food into the house. Jay and Lata entered the house, offered homage to the family deities at the household shrine, offered *namaskar* to the elders of the family and, while the bridegroom's family priest chanted the appropriate mantra, Jay and Lata faced North and viewed the pole star. This ritual implies that the couple will be constant and faithful to each other. The ceremonial part of the marriage was over, and the day-to-day task of living together as husband and wife had already begun.

Before the wedding procession, when people were resting in the afternoon, Appa and Dada, with the help of four servants, had collected all bedding and items not used in the wedding, and asked the servants to take the hand carts to Appa's house. Then they had paid the manager for the use of the hall, paid the cooks, the servers and the servants. All the friends who had helped in the preparation for the wedding were asked to have a simple meal on the day after the wedding. The cooks were to prepare the meal and the women from both the families were to serve the food. After the procession had left, the Brahmin Marriage Hall was not completely deserted, because the cooks and the servants were to stay there overnight.

After their evening meal, Jay and Lata retired to Jay's room, which was on the first floor. His parents and his elder brother and his wife were to occupy the two rooms on the ground floor. Jay was twenty-five and Lata was twenty-one, but their formal education had been 'bookish' and did not include knowledge of how to behave on the wedding night. Lata was shy and modest. Jay was unsure about the sex act.

'Lata,' whispered Jay, 'if I am going to live in Britain, we should not have any children for a few years. I shall probably be able to plan my trip to take place in 1950.'

'I agree with you,' she whispered. 'You will have to take precautions.'

It was pretty much a case of the blind leading the blind. Gently he pulled Lata towards him when they were lying down on the mattress. He had his shirt and loose white pyjama trousers on and she still wore her blouse and sari.

Though fully clothed, their first physical contact bewildered them both. He loosened his pyjama trousers and then lifted her sari and with her help removed her pants. At the sight of her thighs his spirit rose high. He had managed to get a sheath, which he tried to roll on. Lata lay passively, absolutely petrified. They had switched off the light. In the dark he persuaded her to open her thighs so that he could make the connection. His sheathed ego did manage to enter the opening, but before he could push further his eagerness melted. He had to move away and take off the sheath to avoid any accidents. In the dark he was not able to see the disappointment on her face, only hear her long sigh. Both were anxious to learn this new game and looked forward to the next time. The night passed in silence but their curiosity remained sharp. They had become husband and wife but they had a long way to go yet, to become a man and wife.

Step Two

In January 1950, Baba Joshi and his wife, with their two sons and two daughters, were able to overcome the trauma of losing their home in Dhoam, a village to the west of Wai in the river Krishna basin in western India. Although Baba worked as a priest, he had some arable land which was protected under the terms of the land grant made to one of Baba's ancestors for loyal service rendered to the Peshwa rulers of Pune in the closing decade of the eighteenth century. This provision was most fortunate for Baba, because he did not lose the land to the tenant farmer who cultivated it, under the new Land Act passed in 1943 in western India. When the Peshwaship at Pune was abolished by the British in 1818, land grants and other religious donations made by the Peshwas were continued by the new political masters. This land grant had enabled Baba to recover his family's fortunes after the devastating house fires that raged in Dhoam in the first week of February 1948, after the assassination of Mahatma Gandhi.

The origins of this anti-Brahmin movement and caste hatred in Maharashtra in western India could be traced to the year 1713 when Shahu, the grandson of the Maratha King Shivaji, made Balaji Vishvanath Bhat his *panta pradhan* or chief minister. The Sanskrit term faded into the background and the Persian term *peshwa* – a deputy – became well known.

The successors of King Shahu of Satara lacked the ability to control the diverse elements in the kingdom. The capacity of the first Peshwa for military campaigns, for administration, for accounts and for diplomacy was inherited by his son, Bajirao I, his grandson, Balaji known as Nanasaheb, and great-grandson Madhavrao I. They controlled the army and the treasury and directed the energies of adventurous youths towards the expansion of the Maratha kingdom northwards and established Maratha colonies outside Maharashtra at places like Baroda, Dhar, Dewas, Ujjaine, Indore, Nagpur and Gwalior. The rulers of these dependent outposts later formed famous Indian Princely States. They belonged to the dominant Maratha caste who were held together for the benefit of the Maratha Raj by the Peshwa at Pune. The Peshwa was a Chitpavan Brahmin who exercised central control from Pune. Under a strong-willed Peshwa, the Maratha nobles co-operated without hesitation, but when the Peshwa turned out to be weak or a minor, after 1772, the non-Brahmin nobles refused to toe the line. The first four Peshwas expanded the Maratha influence in north India. After Shahu's death in 1749, the Peshwa, on sheer merit and ability, controlled the Maratha state effectively.

The Chitpavan Brahmins who rose to prominence under the Peshwas displayed outstanding qualities and helped the state. But the Brahmins were blamed for losing the Maratha independence in 1818. This deep-seated hatred of Brahmins reared its head in the early decades of the twentieth century. Brahmins were blamed for the many ills of Indian society because they had better intellect, better education and better jobs. Brahmins had to be punished somehow. Brahmins played important roles in many aspects of Indian political social and religious life between 1857 and 1947, but the Brahmin assassin of Mahatma Gandhi gave the dominant caste the excuse they were looking for.

26

In Dhoam village, sixteen houses were set on fire by the well-organised thugs. One of their leaders was involved in the underground anti-British activities in the 1942 'Quit India' movement. He had found shelter in Dhoam, away from the police. Baba Joshi, on many occasions risked arrest by helping that leader with food and clothing in 1942/43. It was like giving milk to a snake, which only increased the venom. That very man led the thugs who set fire to the Brahmin houses in Dhoam, and that same man personally ignited Baba Joshi's house through the venom of hatred. Baba was astounded, speechless and frightened. Along with other Brahmin men, women and children, he fled the disaster area and hid in a field. After the thugs had done their work, they freshened up near the riverbank and left the village. All the Brahmins then emerged from their hiding places and went to the large Vishnu temple near the river.

Baba, his wife, one son and two daughters had a meal of rice and lentils that evening. His elder son, Ashok, was away at college. Baba was angry to see his life's work undone and burnt to ashes by the thugs, who probably got some active support in the village. He had collected many manuscripts of Hindu scriptures, along with texts that were useful for his work as a priest. In his house were stored large cooking utensils, which were used to cook the *prasad* meal for a thousand people at the annual festival of Narasimha Vishnu. Apart from the loss of personal material possessions, and the brass and copper utensils belonging to the temple trust, the loss of manuscripts and books was deeply felt by him.

As Baba had the ownership title to the land, he was entitled to receive sixty per cent of the produce from the tenant farmer. Thus he had a regular income from the fields as well as from his work as a priest, which enabled him to recover from the trauma of the house fires. Some victims of the house fires were not so fortunate. They had to wait in crushing penury for ten or fifteen years until their sons had got some post-secondary school education and found a job. One thing was common to all the victims, they realised that they were not wanted in the village. Along with some other families, Baba left the village and rented a house in the neighbouring town of Wai, where his younger children could attend schools.

By January 1950, Baba's elder son, Ashok, had managed to get a science degree after four years at a college in Pune. He had decided to seek employment in the new State Transport department. He applied for a lower level managerial post and having got through the interview successfully, was appointed as an assistant manager at the ST Depot at Satara. Ashok was now twenty-five, he had a fairly good education and a job. Baba had had a long talk with him about marriage to a suitable Brahmin young lady from a Chitpavan family. Baba contacted three marriage brokers in Wai who had contacts in Pune, Satara, Karad and Sangli. Nearly a month went by before Baba got any response to his enquiries. In fact there were two young women whose horoscopes matched with Ashok's. One was from Pune, the other from Sangli.

Baba and Ashok and his mother studied the letter that came with the horoscope from Pune. The girl was called Meera. She was born into a well-to-do Chitpavan family. The father was a lawyer. Meera had a younger brother who was studying at a well-known college in Pune, and she herself had obtained an MA degree in literature, mainly Sanskrit and Marathi literature.

'Well, Ashok,' said Baba, 'what do you think of this young lady as your future wife?'

'In spite of the favourable horoscopes, I think there are two factors here which would create discord in the future.'

'What are you saying?' asked Bai, his mother.

'I think the family is very rich, and if the young lady is used to a very comfortable lifestyle, she would not be very happy in our family.'

'What is the other factor?' asked Baba.

'She has an MA degree while I only have a BSc. I shall not be at ease in that situation.'

Baba and Bai considered their son's argument and agreed that the girl from Pune would not be a suitable daughter-in-law for them.

'Right, Ashok,' said Baba. 'I shall write a letter to Meera's parents to say that we are considering other prospective brides and that they should look elsewhere for a husband for their daughter. Now let us consider the other letter, which is from Sangli.'

'Aho, why don't you read the letter aloud!' said Bai to her husband, without saying his name. It is a widely held belief and practice in upper-caste Hindu families that married women should not utter their husband's first name, because by doing so they shorten his life. Hindus are often criticised for being superstitious, but people from other climes and cultures and other religious traditions also have their particular superstitions, which are equally mysterious. Human beings the world over seem to fear the unknown. In western India married women in Brahmin families usually refer to their husbands as 'him' and when they wish to draw his attention, they start the sentence with the vocative 'Aho' – meaning 'respected sir'.

While Baba was silently reading the letter from Sangli, Bai repeated her question: 'Aho, why don't you read the letter aloud?'

Baba now began to read the letter, which was written in Marathi, the regional language of Maharashtra State in India.

Greetings and *namaskar* to Mr and Mrs Babarao Joshi

of Wai. Our family priest received a letter from the marriage broker in Wai, which gave the essential information about your family and about your elder son Ashok.

I am hereby giving relevant information about our family in Sangli and our marriageable daughter Manjiri. Although my given name is Narayan, I am generally known by my nickname Nana and my wife is called Aaee – mother. Manjiri is our eldest daughter; we have another daughter called Kaveri and a son, who is in the matriculation class. He is called Vishnu. Our family name is Goray. Our financial position is not very strong so we shall not be able to give any dowry.

I think you, your wife and son Ashok should come to Sangli for two or three days to meet Manjiri and the rest of the family. This visit will give you a clear indication of our financial position. Consider it a break from your normal routine. We can have a full and frank discussion about the possible marriage alliance in this personal and informal visit.

Do please write and tell me the time of your possible visit.

Sincerely, *Nana Goray.*

Both Ashok and Bai were pleased to get that invitation.

'Well, Baba,' said Ashok, 'I think it would be a good idea to visit Sangli and meet the Goray family.'

'Yes, I think so, too,' replied Baba. That evening he wrote a short letter to Nana Goray, which he was going to post the next day.

Greetings and *namaskar* to Nanasaheb Goray and family. We were pleased to receive your letter of invitation. Ashok, my wife Bai and myself will come

30

to Sangli in the third week of January. I have one son and two daughters younger than Ashok. They are busy with their school work so they will stay at Wai, being looked after by my widowed aunt, while we come to Sangli for three days. We shall travel to Satara Road station, where we shall catch the train to Sangli. We plan to start our journey on the Tuesday of the third week of the month.

Looking forward to meeting you,

Sincerely, *Baba Joshi*

On the Tuesday in the third week – Baba, Bai and Ashok travelled by the State Transport bus to the railway station and boarded the train for Sangli. After a long and tiring journey they were met at Sangli station by Nana Goray. After introductions and greetings, they walked to Nana's house.

Nana's wife, Aaee, welcomed the guests and said that she would make tea while the guests freshened up. Twenty minutes later, Manjiri and Aaee brought the tea and refreshments to the front room of their small house. Ashok and Manjiri met but they only exchanged smiles and not words. While the guests were having tea, Kaveri, Nana's younger daughter, and Vishnu, his son, came home from school. After freshening up, the younger children came to the sitting room and made *namaskars* – by bowing low with palms held in front of them. Baba, instinctively, spoke a blessing in Sanskrit – 'May you be blessed with a long life.' Baba and Ashok learned that Manjiri had obtained a BA degree in languages, which included English along with Marathi and Hindi. Kaveri told them that she was studying at Willingdon College for a BSc, while Vishnu was to appear for the matriculation examination that year.

'Babarao,' said Nana, 'did you lose your house and

possessions in the anti-Brahmin riots and burning in February 1948?'

'Yes,' replied Baba, 'it was a very frightening experience. There were sixteen houses set on fire in our village called Dhoam, which is five miles to the west of Wai. The most hurtful memory is of losing my collection of old manuscripts of religious texts and many printed books about Hindu religious rituals. The political agitators were out to punish Brahmins for keeping the non-Brahmin masses away from primary and secondary education. Yet, the *goondas* – thugs – were quite happy in their ignorance to burn books and manuscripts, the sources of knowledge.'

Then Baba described in much detail the events of the particular day in 1948 when the Brahmin men, women and children in Dhoam were made refugees in the village where some families had lived for over 185 years.

After the evening meal, the four women used the inner room as their bedroom, while the four men used the sitting room for their night's rest.

'We'll go for a long walk in the city tomorrow morning,' said Nana, 'so that you can see the places where there are still signs of that fire damage.'

The following morning after ablutions and tea, Nana, Vishnu, Baba and Ashok went for a leisurely walk in Sangli. They came across a large gap between two houses.

'Here,' said Nana, 'we had the finest bookshop in the city, owned by a hardworking Chitpavan Brahmin. The thugs were from the neighbouring city of Kolhapur. There used to be, and probably still are, the wrestling gyms called *talims*. They were the training centres for the *goondas*. They were taught physical culture to keep fit and the anti-Brahmin hatred was poured into their very souls by the specifically selected political activists.

'Those *goondas* came with phosphorus sticks and paraffin oil cans. They broke the doors and windows, toppled the

32

bookshelves, made a large pile of books in the middle of the shop and set it alight. The owners barely had time to escape from their flat above the shop.

'The gangs of thugs were well organised. They selected their targets in advance. Many, if not most, house, shop and printing press fires were started at the same time. There was no escape. When the *goondas* had ignited the private houses of Brahmins, they turned their skills on the small industries started and owned by Chitpavans in the city. The chief of Sangli was a Chitpavan who encouraged industrial expansion.'

Now Baba and Nana with their sons had come to the site of the finest textile mill in Sangli. Most of the workers were non-Brahmins. They had joined the *goondas* with enthusiasm. When the mill was set on fire and the machinery was broken, the workers made themselves jobless.

'The tragic situation arose when the workers bit the hand that fed them,' said Nana. 'The owner of the mill was a Chitpavan Brahmin who had started his textile enterprise in 1914. He was devastated to see his 34 years' work undone by the mindless morons in a couple of days.'

'Nana,' asked Baba, 'tell me, how much loss was suffered by the Brahmins in Sangli? Has anyone calculated the cost?'

'No exact figures are available. In the Sangli State alone some 23 million rupees' worth of damage was done, which was even more than in the neighbouring non-Brahmin state.'

'I have read reports of the burning that took place in Bombay, Nagpur, Pune and other cities, towns and villages in Bombay province in February 1948,' said Baba. 'The total damage to Brahmin property is estimated at 12 crores of rupees, which is 120 million rupees. In the northern area of Belgaun district alone fire damage was 10 million rupees.'

After seeing the signs of the house fires, Baba and Nana returned to Nana's house, and when they had enjoyed a simple midday meal of rice, unleavened bread made of jowar flour, spiced lentils and vegetables, the visitors from Wai rested for a couple of hours.

Bai had helped with the food preparations for about an hour. During that time she made a mental note of the contents of the kitchen. She found that the cooking and eating utensils of the Goray family were of similar quality and standard as their own in Wai. Aaee and Manjiri wore four gold bangles each, while the younger daughter wore only two gold bangles, along with glass ones. The saris worn by the Goray women were attractive without being expensive. Manjiri proudly told Bai that all their saris came from the Gajanan Mill, which was severely damaged in the 1948 fires.

At four in the afternoon, Aaee made tea and asked everyone to come to the sitting room.

'Well, Ashok,' began Nana, 'you have seen how we live here. We are certainly not rich, but we are not living a hand-to-mouth existence. Kaveri and Vishnu have won scholarships, which helps me with their education.'

'Ashokrao,' said Aaee, 'you have met Manjiri. Why don't you two ask each other important questions? We shall sit here and listen.'

'Ashokrao,' said Manjiri, 'I like you and I would like to be your wife, but if we are married, will you force your ideas, likes and dislikes on me like an old-fashioned Hindu husband?'

'No, Manjiri,' replied Ashok. 'I will give you freedom of choice to express your likes and dislikes as long as we want to remain husband and wife. Will you take a job after marriage? It will help me budget our household expenses.'

'Yes, I would like to get a job, probably some office work,' replied Manjiri.

'Well, Nanasaheb,' said Baba, 'the younger generation appear to have more or less settled their future lifestyle. It would give Bai and me a good deal of pleasure to have Manju as our daughter-in-law.'

'We are happy to hear your words.' Nana and Aaee spoke at the same time.

'Before we decide on when and how elaborately the marriage will be performed, I would like to make some observations,' said Ashok.

'Yes, go ahead,' responded Nana Goray.

'Let me refer to the events of February 1948. It is true that there was much anti-Brahmin, particularly anti-Chitpavan rioting, looting, burning and in one particular instance, murder, in many villages and also in cities like Nagpur, Bombay and Pune but the deep-seated poisonous hatred of Chitpavan by the dominant Maratha caste was displayed glaringly in Satara district and in the Kolhapur-Sangli-Miraj areas. Here the Chitpavans were most hated. I have been thinking about the future and I have come to the conclusion that I would not like to live in, say, Dhoam-Wai area or indeed Sangli-Miraj districts, where I shall experience the hatred at every turn.'

'But, Ashok,' said Baba, 'where would you like to settle after you get married?'

'Temporarily, I shall live in Satara, now that I have got a job in the new State Transport department, but it will be temporary. Eventually I would like to leave India and settle in Britain.'

'What sort of job would you get there?'

'Well, I could get a job with the British Railways Authority. I am not going immediately. I shall need to save a lot of money, but if I plan carefully, I could be going to London in, say, 1958.'

'Ashokrao,' said Aaee, 'have you discussed this idea before?'

'No, this is the first time I am speaking about it.'

'Will Manju be prepared to settle in London?'

'Well, Manju?' asked Ashok. 'Do you like the idea of settling abroad?'

'This is quite a novel idea. Yes, I would like to settle in London, if that is what you are planning to do.'

'Good,' said Ashok, rather relieved to hear Manju's readiness to travel abroad. 'Now we can consider the mode of our marriage ceremony.'

'Babarao,' said Nana, 'since Ashok and Manju are thinking of going abroad in the near future, I think we should have an inexpensive wedding ceremony. That way both families could save a lot of money. Then we could make our contribution to their foreign travel.'

'Yes, I agree entirely,' replied Baba. 'The marriage will be performed here in Sangli, that being the bride's place. We shall travel from Wai. There will be six of us in the immediate Joshi family and I would like to invite two couples who are our very close friends. So the bridegroom's party will consist of ten persons.'

'Well,' responded Nana, 'we shall follow the same pattern. We shall have not more than twelve persons on the bride's side. This does not include the priests, the cooks and other helpers.'

'There are auspicious days for weddings in the month of *phalgun* (February–March). This will give us enough time to make arrangements,' said Baba. 'We are staying one more day here. We would like to visit the Raja's Palace in Sangli before we go back to Wai.'

'Yes certainly,' replied Nana, 'we can do that tomorrow.'

Baba and Bai were pleased that the important matter of Ashok's marriage was settled without many obstacles. They both thought that Manju would make a very suitable wife for Ashok.

Thursday of that week was the third day of the Joshi

family's visit to Sangli. Three persons from Wai and three hosts from Sangli set out to visit the Palace of the Patwardhan Rajas of Sangli. Only the public rooms, such as the main Durbar Hall, the family deity's shrine, the stables and the grounds were open to visitors. The private apartments were occupied by the Raja's family. Baba was impressed by the ornate Durbar Hall, and Nana was able to provide some historical background to the rise of the Patwardhan States in southern Maharashtra.

In the first decade of the eighteenth century a devout ancestor of the Patwardhan family migrated from Ratnagiri district and took up appointment as a family priest to the Chitpavan Raja of Ichalkaranji. Balaji, the first Peshwa of King Shahu of Satara – the grandson of the Maratha King Shivaji – heard of this priest and kept contact with him. Later the sons of this devout priest took service under the Peshwa rulers of Pune. Although Brahmins, they displayed valour in various campaigns under the Peshwas Bajirao and Balaji Nana. For this service to the Maratha State these Patwardhans were given land grants in the fertile valley of the river Krishna. Their fief bordered on the Maratha Rajas of Kolhapur, who were the descendants of the junior branch of Chatrapati. The Peshwas placed their own faithful servants and friends as a check on the activities of the Kolhapur Rajas. The seeds of Brahmin–Maratha caste hatred were sown in around 1763 under the fourth Peshwa, Madhavrao senior.

When India was about to become independent, there were eighteen Princely States in southern Maharashtra, out of which ten were ruled by Brahmin families. Two were ruled by Deshasthas, a sub-caste from the plateau (Bhor and Aundh), and the remaining eight by Chitpavan Brahmins who originated from the coastal areas. Ramdurga was ruled by the Bhave family and seven were ruled by the Pawardhan family. Of these Miraj and Sangli were forward looking, and home to industries started and owned by Chitpavan Brahmins like Velankar, Bhide and Dandekar. During the anti-Chitpavan riots the industries and private houses were set on fire. Fortunately, the palace was left unharmed.

Baba expressed his gratitude to Nana for showing him the palace. After midday meal, Baba related his experiences of the misplaced patriotic activities of the Congress agitators around Wai and the north Satara district during the 1942 "Quit India" movement.

'Nansaheb, as you have no doubt read in the Maratha history, there are very few historical buildings left in Maharashtra, because there was much resistance to British rule right up to 1818. The wife of Peshwa Balaji Nana came from the Raste family, who had some land grants and grand buildings at Wai. The Rastes, being closely related to the Peshwa family at Pune, were very proud of their connection and had built a special guest house palace to welcome the Peshwa Madhavrao junior to Wai. The building dated from the 1780s and was situated in the western ward called Ganga-puri. They had constructed eight large wooden gates which could be closed and locked to make the guest house secure and safe.

'When the Peshwarship was abolished by the British administration in 1818, the various buildings belonging to the Raste family survived. The guest house palace eventually housed the sub-judge's civil court at Wai from the start of the twentieth century. During the "Quit India" movement, which was directed towards upsetting the British rule in Satara district, the Congress agitators set fire to the civil court building at Wai in early 1943. Through the efforts of many persons, half the building was saved, but the entire court records were in ashes. The British Governor at Bombay and the district officer at Satara promptly decided to shift the Wai civil court twenty miles

38

away to Satara, the district town. The British were not in any way inconvenienced by this mindless patriotic act of the Congress agitators. Who suffered by this act of vandalism? The non-Brahmin farmer litigants, the lawyers practising in that court and the various witnesses needed for the land lawsuits. They all had to travel by the "court-special" buses to Satara every day and the litigants had to pay the travelling expenses. The biggest loss was suffered by the future Maharashtra State in that they were deprived of a historical building. The agitators learnt their burning skills in the "Quit India" movement. One of the leaders had taken shelter at Dhoam. I had personally helped him with food and clothing for nearly two years while he avoided arrest. That same man led the thugs in the Dhoam fires and he himself set our house alight. These underground agitators became "respectable" politicians after Independence. My kindness was repaid in the ashes of my rare manuscripts. I am not at all surprised to hear that Ashok wishes to emigrate to Britain soon after marriage.'

The Goray family were visibly moved by Baba's narration.

The members of these two Chitpavan families were light-complexioned and had grey-green eyes, which are a typical distinctive characteristic of the Chitpavan Brahmins of western India.

On Friday of that week in January 1950, Baba, Bai and Ashok returned to Wai, looking forward to their second visit to Sangli for the wedding ceremony. Two days later, Ashok took up his job in the State Transport Depot at Satara.

Towards the end of January 1950, Nana Goray consulted his family priest about the auspicious days for Ashok and Manjiri's wedding. The priest looked up the tables printed in the Hindu Almanac for the Shaka Era and advised

Nana Goray that the sixth lunar date in the second week of April of that year was an auspicious day for marriage and was more suitable for Manjiri. The next day Nana posted a letter to Baba Joshi and asked whether the suggested date would meet his approval. By a lucky coincidence, Baba Joshi had consulted the Hindu Lunisolar Almanac and had felt that the sixth lunar date would be suitable for Ashok's marriage to Manjiri. When he received the letter from Sangli he showed it to his wife and pointed out the coincidence. Baba and Bai were happy to say 'yes' to the suggested day for the wedding ceremony, and Baba wrote to Nana Goray to confirm the proposed day for the ceremony. He also posted a letter to Ashok to give him the details of the arrangements. As soon as the relevant information was received by Nana Goray in Sangli, both the families began preparations for the forthcoming marriage in the second week of April.

When Ashok received his father's letter he was glad to read the news of the proposed wedding day. He mentioned it to the ST Depot manager in conversation that very afternoon. The manager, who was a Brahmin, though not a Chitpavan, congratulated Ashok and asked whether the marriage would be performed in Wai.

'No, it will take place at Sangli since my future wife, Manjiri Goray, comes from that city.'

'How many of you will travel from Wai to Sangli?' asked the manager.

'Ten altogether. Six from the Joshi family and four close friends,' explained Ashok.

'If I may suggest, Ashok, you should travel by the ST service from Wai to Sangli. It would be very convenient and, of course, as an employee you would get a discount on the group fares.'

'I had not considered bus travel, but it would be very convenient. Thank you for your suggestion.'

The next day Ashok wrote to his father and reported his conversation with the depot manager and mentioned the discount fares for the group ticket to Sangli. He added that he would book the return ticket so that they could leave Wai two days before the day of the wedding, and do their return journey from Sangli on the third day after the wedding. He further added that there would be two additional passengers for the return journey since Manjiri would be accompanied by her younger sister, Kaveri, as a chaperon.

Baba Joshi was very happy to get the information from Ashok, and passed it on to Nana Goray.

In the second week of February, when Ashok had two days' leave, Baba, Bai and Ashok travelled by ST bus to Pune to buy saris, dhotis and shirt pieces for various members of both families. After their shopping they had lunch at a well-known vegetarian restaurant and returned to Wai by the late afternoon service. Baba was happy that they had managed to buy gifts of clothes to celebrate Ashok's marriage.

Nana Goray had hired a small marriage hall, with four double rooms on the first floor, which were to be used by the guests and the hosts.

The wedding altar had been prepared in the courtyard and the wedding feast was to be held in the large reception hall on the ground floor. Nana had arranged everything needed for a small wedding ceremony and had kept the expenses to a minimum.

Baba Joshi's party was welcomed by the Goray family when they reached Sangli in the afternoon. Baba saw the arrangements made by Nana and expressed his appreciation with much enthusiasm. After refreshments, Nana informed Ashok that the following morning four young students were to call on Ashok to have an informal chat. Ashok was intrigued by this news and looked forward to making new friends in Sangli.

41

In the morning of the day before the wedding ceremony, four bright young students called at the marriage hall to meet Ashok.

'I am Manohar and my friends are called Arvind, Rajendra and Madhav. You must be wondering, Ashok, why we have come here on a day when you would be very busy with your wedding preparations.'

'Yes,' responded Ashok, 'I am anxious to know the reason.'

'Rajendra's sister is a family friend of your future wife,' began Manohar, 'and through her we have learned that you are thinking of leaving India and will probably settle in Britain. Is that so?'

'Yes, that is my intention.'

'Good, all four of us are also thinking along the same lines. So we thought we could have a chat and find out what things we have in common.'

'Why don't you each say a few words about your family, education and your future plans,' suggested Ashok.

'I'll start, if I may,' said Manohar. 'I come from Jamkhandi. I was born in a Chitpavan family, and although there was no fire damage done to Brahmin houses in Jamkhandi during the February riots after the assassination of Gandhi, there has been and always will be deep-seated hatred of Brahmins in general and of the Chitpavans in particular. At present I am in medical college training to be a doctor; and after qualilfying, I am thinking of emigrating to Britain.'

'I was born in a Chitpavan Brahmin family in Ichalkaranji,' said Arvind. 'For over a hundred years the Brahmins in that Princely State have been subjected to hatred by the dominant Maratha population in Kolhapur State. There has been keen rivalry between the Brahmin prince of Ichalkaranji and the Maratha prince of Kolhapur, since that Brahmin State has been a feudatory of Kolhapur for a long time. During the anti-Chitpavan riots and arson after the Mahatma was shot by a Chitpavan intellectual from Pune, enormous damage was done to Brahmin houses in Kolhapur and Ichalkaranji, but the damage was a little less severe than that experienced by the Brahmins in Sangli. Our house was reduced to ashes. I am training to be a civil engineer in Sangli and have decided to escape this persecution by emigrating to Britain. I have no definite plans as yet, but it will be as soon as possible after I graduate.'

'Arvind,' said Ashok, 'our house in Dhoam, near Wai, was also destroyed by fire. So we have a lot in common. How about you, Rajendra?'

'As you will have probably gathered, I was born in a Chitpavan Brahmin family in Sangli, and my sister is a friend of your future wife. Manjiri has visited our house many times. Allow me to congratulate you on your choice. To continue, I am in the same medical college as Manohar and our family house was completely burned down during the 1948 anti-Chitpavan riots. That is the main reason why I am going to try and go to Britain. I realise that there will be anti-Indian prejudice in Britain, but that will not be as virulent as the hatred displayed by the dominant Maratha caste in Bombay Province against the Chitpavan Brahmins. Now that the non-Brahmins have become the political masters in Bombay, Brahmins should emigrate to escape the poisonous policies now being put into operation.'

'I am slightly different,' said Madhav, 'since I was born in a Deshastha Brahmin family in a place called Narsobachi Wadi, not far from Kolhapur. My father was a temple priest there when the Talim Sangh thugs from Kolhapur attacked our town in large numbers. We were terrified and feared for our lives. We had to leave our houses, possessions, books, manuscripts and run, as the trained

43

mobs set almost all the houses on fire. Some priests suffered physical injury and we all suffered the verbal abuse and foul language. Our family also lost the shelter and we became homeless. I am at present studying to be an accountant. After my degree course, I am hoping to go to London as soon as I can get some money together; some of it will be a long-term loan from other Brahmin friends. Although the main target was the Chitpavan community, other Brahmins also lost their houses.'

'Not only other Brahmins,' said Arvind, 'but also some non-Brahmins. The biggest target in Kolhapur was the film studio, which was actually owned by a Maratha, but other "pure" Marathas considered him "brahmanised" and hence polluted. So the Chitpavans and their friends experienced fire damage and homelessness in that anti-Brahmin storm.'

Ashok offered his unexpected visitors tea and snacks and invited them to attend his wedding the next day.

'Before we go, Ashok,' said Manohar, 'tell us what your line of work is.'

'I have got a job as an assistant ST Depot Manager at Satara. Soon after I went there I learned an interesting story. In Satara district most primary school teachers were Brahmins. There was a non-Brahmin politicised agitator called Bhaurao who was determined to break this Brahmin influence in schools in order to emancipate the dominant Maratha caste through education. His slogan was "Non-Brahmins should be taught by non-Brahmin teachers" and to that end he started primary schools for non-Brahmins. Ironically, Bhaurao was helped with ideas and money by two prominent Chitpavan Brahmins at the start of his project.

'By 1948, there were many schools in the district where non-Brahmin pupils were taught by non-Brahmin teachers. This financial help for the endeavour, from Chitpavan

Brahmins, was repaid with the ashes of Brahmin houses all over Satara district, where nearly a thousand houses were burned.'

The four guests felt an affinity towards Ashok when they left with a promise to attend the wedding the next day. And after hearing the horror stories of the young men, Ashok was even more resolved to leave western India and try his luck in Britain.

After the young visitors had left, Ashok inspected the wedding plinth in the courtyard of the hall and had a long chat with his father, when he narrated the conversation he had with Manohar and his three friends.

'Well, Ashok,' said Baba, 'I think you will benefit in the long run by going to live and work in Britain. Remember that you are going to find prejudice no matter where you go, but I am sure the anti-Indian prejudice in Britain will be less severe than what the Brahmins are facing now and are likely to face in the future in western India.'

'Yes, I realise that,' responded Ashok, 'but all the same, I am going to do my best to go to London as soon as I save the necessary money.'

After lunch, everyone had a rest to combat the midday heat of late April. In the late afternoon Ashok and Vishnu Goray, his future brother-in-law, went out for a leisurely stroll. Although Vishnu was in his final year in the high school, Ashok found him quite mature in his conversation and manner. He learned from Vishnu that Manjiri had mentioned Ashok's name many times in the two and a half months since the betrothal in January. That bit of information pleased Ashok. He himself had thought of her many times, but of course he did not say a word to Vishnu about it.

As they returned to the marriage hall, Vishnu said to Ashok, 'I am going to enjoy twisting your ear tomorrow during the wedding service.'

45

Ashok gave a hearty laugh and patted Vishnu on the back.

The wedding day dawned bright and hot. The May heat seemed to have begun a couple of weeks earlier than usual. Although the most auspicious moment was just after ten in the morning, everyone was up by five. By seven they had completed their toilet visits and brushed their teeth before bathing. The cooks had been busy in the preparation of various ingredients before cooking the feast lunch. When everyone had bathed, the cooks made tea so that all men and women could refresh themselves before getting involved in the ceremony.

The family priest of Nana Goray arrived with his assistant and started getting the altar ready. Three seating boards were placed side by side on the plinth. A small square table was used to place the Murtis – consecrated images – of the god Ganesha and the Mother Goddess and two copper vessels with water representing the holy rivers of Hinduism. Betel leaves, betel nuts and copper coins were placed before the Murtis, and five leaves were placed on each water vessel before putting a coconut on it. Various articles of worship were placed on a couple of trays. A metal tin was used to light the fire for the marriage *homa* to make offering to Agni, the God of Fire.

Baba discussed a couple of changes in the usual order of the service with Nana Goray and the priest. It was agreed that the Joshi family would first offer worship to the god Ganesha, the goddess and the river deities and would withdraw into the reception hall while the Goray family offered similar worship. When the bride had gone into a small side room for her private worship and prayers, Ashok and his parents would stand just outside the main door of the marriage hall, where they would be formally welcomed by Manjiri's parents. This *seemanta puja* used to be performed at the boundary of the bride's village in the distant past, but modern modification enables the bride's parents to perform this 'welcoming ceremony of the bridegroom' at the entrance to the marriage hall where the wedding ceremony is celebrated.

After welcoming Ashok at the door, Nana Goray and his wife gave him some honey yoghurt to sweeten the welcome. When the daughter was being given in marriage, Ashok had to touch Manjiri's right shoulder with his right hand to indicate his acceptance. As he touched her shoulder he felt her skin respond with a momentary pleasure. Since the three generations of the ancestors of the couple had to be mentioned three times by name, Ashok had a chance to touch his bride's shoulder twice more, and, on both occasions, he felt the same pleasure coming from her skin on to the palm of his hand. When they were standing face to face to express their three wishes, Ashok noticed a little twinkle of friendship in Manjiri's eyes and, fleetingly, he remembered Vishnu's words from the previous evening's conversation. Immediately after the 'giving of the daughter in marriage' ritual, she had asked Ashok to promise her that he would be moderate in the performance of his *dharma* – social and religious duty – his *artha* – the earning of a living by honest work – and his *kama* – the enjoyment of the good things in life. She had looked deeply into his eyes while demanding the promise. He had fixed his eyes on hers to convey his sincerity.

Had she really been thinking of him in the previous two months as he had been secretly thinking of her, was a passing question in his mind. When the bride and the bridegroom were tying a turmeric root with a soft cotton thread to each other's wrists, both enjoyed a slightly longer touch with the other's skin, and again a feeling of pleasure and comfort passed between them.

Ashok tied the marriage necklace of black beads round Manjiri's neck with a sense of long-term commitment. He had to take his bride's right hand in his right hand and repeat the vedic mantra after the priest. He felt that Manjiri was conveying a need for physical closeness through wordless pressure of her hand. He was rather embarrassed by his involuntary physical response to that wordless pressure. Luck provided a little longer interval before the next ritual, during which he was able to compose his feelings and get ready to make the various oblations to Agni. As he poured a spoonful of ghee after each mantra, Manjiri touched his right hand with an intentionally firm touch of her right hand. Now Ashok was convinced that Manjiri had indeed been thinking of him since the betrothal.

After the main marriage *homa*, the worship of the God of Fire, they had to make offerings of roasted rice to Agni, then holding hands they walked round the fire and in the third part of the ritual, she had to put her right foot on a stone slab and symbolically be ready to stand firm as a rock to defend her and her new family's honour. Vishnu now twisted Ashok's right ear to remind Ashok of his duty to Manjiri, and Ashok gave Vishnu ten rupees. As they circumambulated the fire thrice, Manjiri held Ashok's hand with firm willingness, which made him happy.

At the seven steps ritual, after each mantra and each step Manjiri made a promise that she would indeed support Ashok in all his lawful undertakings. After the 'giving of the daughter in marriage' ritual, they were merely bride and bridegroom. As they performed the successive rituals in the ceremony their status gradually changed and their commitment to each other increased. After the seventh mantra in the seven steps ritual, as they vowed to be friend and companion to each other for life, they became husband and wife.

The priest sprinkled them with water as he spoke the appropriate mantras and prayed that they may be blessed with strength, riches, success and food. After they had prayed to Agni for various blessings, Manjiri's parents brought the ceremony to a close. Now the guests were ready to give the newly-weds their blessings in the form of rice as the verses of blessing were sung by both the priests. At the end of each verse, the guests showered them with a few grains of rice.

When the screen of shawl was removed from between them, they were able to see each other. A little water from the blessed vessels was applied to their eyes to bring them blessings of the river deities.

Ashok smiled at his wife and Manjiri smiled at her husband and wordlessly they conveyed their happiness with each other. The four young students who had visited Ashok the previous day had indeed attended the wedding ceremony and spoke their congratulations to the newly-weds.

After the bride's father and the officiating priest had given their blessing, the newly-weds sat down on the wedding plinth and received presents and good wishes from the guests. Both Baba Joshi and Nana Goray gave a token return gift of either a sari or a shirt piece to everyone who had given a present to Ashok and Manjiri. When the gift exchange interval was over, Ashok asked Manjiri's sister Kaveri to arrange some tea and snacks for them.

'Manju,' said Ashok, 'I am very happy to have you as my wife, friend and partner.'

'I am very lucky to be your wife,' responded Manjiri, without speaking her husband's first name.

'Why don't you say my first name?' asked Ashok.

'It is our general custom. I shall say "Aho" when I want to draw your attention in the presence of other people, and when we are alone I shall whisper your first name.'

He held her hand and smiled, looking deep into her eyes. She looked into his eyes, comforted by his hand in hers, and smiled at him. Kaveri brought them refreshments and their private moment vanished.

After having tea and snacks together, the newly-weds had to part in order to prepare for the feast lunch. Although the number of persons for lunch was not very large, the food preparation and serving had to be of a high standard. Since the wedding ceremony arrangements are normally the responsibility of the bride's family, Nana Goray had asked two of his close friends to see to the seating arrangements in the main reception hall. He had also asked the cooks to prepare mango pulp and purees as the main sweet dish for lunch. Manjiri had to change into an expensive sari and Ashok had to wear a yellow silk dhoti for the feast lunch.

The newly-weds occupied two seating boards side by side in the middle of the main row. Lunch was served just after noon. Halfway through the meal, Ashok and Manjiri had to feed a morsel of the main sweet to each other. When the time came, there was utter silence. The servers stopped at one end of the dining hall. Ashok fed Manjiri half a puree with sweetened mango pulp and announced to the gathering that he was happy with Manju. When Manjiri fed Ashok, she spoke his name rather cleverly included in a rhyming couplet. Many people expressed their approval of the rhyme by saying 'well done' in Marathi, the main language in that part of Bombay province. Everyone ate with relish, which pleased both families. Special paan made with betel leaves and aromatic ingredients was given to everyone after lunch as a digestive aid.

Since the bridegroom lived many miles away, there were no special post-wedding ceremonies at Sangli. These were to be performed when the Joshi family with the new daughter-in-law returned to Wai. The afternoon was a time for rest for all. Baba Joshi's family were to stay at Sangli one more day. Nana and Baba had quietly made special sleeping arrangements so that the newly-weds could have complete privacy in one of the double rooms in the marriage hall. Ashok and Manjiri were rather thrilled to learn about it. Both families agreed that in the late afternoon, everyone was to visit the local Ganesha temple so that Ashok and Manjiri could view the murti and offer homage to the deity in thanksgiving for their good fortune.

The cooks had prepared plain rice and spiced lentils for the evening meal, which was welcomed by all. Soon afterwards, Manjiri changed into a cotton sari, had a wash and went to their bedroom, where Ashok had already gone. As Manjiri came into the room, Ashok approached her and held her hand. Then he closed and locked the door. He pulled Manju towards him and embraced her.

'Hello, Manju,' he said in a muffled tone.

'Hello, Ashok,' she whispered.

He held her close with his left arm and could feel her young breasts in close contact with his chest. He felt her back with his right hand and gradually his hand went lower until it rested on her right buttock. Manjiri had her hands round Ashok's neck. As she felt his hand on her behind, she pushed herself forward, which brought her nether region against his secret assets. Thus encouraged by that wordless pressure, Ashok began to feel her globes with firmness and tenderness, paying attention first to the right one and then to the left one in turn. They rested their chins on each other's shoulders.

I want to put my mouth against his, thought Manjiri.

I want to contact her lips with my lips, thought Ashok.

Manju moved her head backward without releasing his neck from her arms. Ashok made the same movement and looked at her. Their mouths were like magnets to the other, but their noses were in the way. Instinct guided Manjiri to tilt her head slightly sideways and search for Ashok's mouth. Ashok responded and slowly their mouths met. She had never kissed any man in her young life. He was equally ignorant of lip contact. It was a case of the blind groping the blind.

Once Ashok had put his lips to Manju's lips he remained still. Manju gently pressed her lips against his lips and both experienced a new sensation. Ashok now put his arms round her body and embraced her firmly. Manjiri did the same, moving her arms downwards till her hands rested on Ashok's back. This novel and first ever experience of kissing the beloved's mouth gradually increased their physical desire.

Ashok had formed a vague notion in his head that his secret part needed to be pushed inside his wife's secret opening. But how to find that opening and how to control the intense throbbing of his pointer were two big question marks in his mind as he stood in deep embrace.

Manjiri had gleaned from bits of conversations which she had overheard in her college common room that a bride on her wedding night has to suffer intrusion into her secret passage and a lot of tearing pain with perhaps some blood before she becomes a woman. As Ashok's pointer began to grow hard, she could feel it very close to her secret opening through his baggy pyjamas and her thin cotton sari. Fear gripped her body as she began to imagine what was going to happen soon. Hindu society in 1950 kept young men and women totally ignorant of the physical side of marriage. In the cities, young men became aware that there are methods which a man has to employ to prevent pregnancies in the early months of married life. Ashok had obtained a couple of rubbers, which he had placed under the pillow. He now indicated without words that he and Manju should lie down on the mattress on the floor. He released her from his embrace and gradually they lowered themselves down on to the mattress.

In that position his body relaxed somewhat but the tension in his pointer increased. He undid the cord of his pyjama trousers and began to remove them slowly. It turned out to be rather tricky since his stiff pointer was hindering the operation.

When he was free of his thin pyjama trousers, he gently lifted Manju's sari up to her waistline. He took one rubber contraceptive, opened the cover and managed to roll it on to his pointer. He whispered to Manju that she should now remove her undies, lie flat on her back and widen her thighs. As soon as Manju followed his instruction, he went in between her widened thighs and rested on his knees, getting his covered pointer as close as possible to her secret passage. Manjiri was lying still, with eyes shut, gritting her teeth as Ashok moved a little forward. Now he could feel his pointer entering her damp passage. He put his hands under her soft behind and lifted it slightly and at the same time pushed his pointer hard into Manju's secret opening. He felt a little resistance and heard Manju making wincing sounds. He increased the pressure and pushed harder. Manjiri was emitting suppressed cries as she experienced tearing pain in her passage and felt a bloated sensation as Ashok had managed to lodge his hard pointer deep in her opening. The severe friction generated in the operation brought on Ashok's moment and his life-making fluid flowed into the rubber covering. The whole venture did not last for more than two or three minutes, and as his energy drained, his pointer softened and slipped out. Instinctively Manju pulled a bit of her sari down to cover her opening and pressed it with her hands on her passage, partly to dull the pain and partly to mop up the moisture she felt oozing from between

53

her thighs. Ashok moved away, pulled off the used contraceptive and using his pyjama trousers mopped up the sticky fluid from his pointer and surrounding area.

He lay down beside Manju and gently stroked her face, arms and back. 'Did I hurt you much?' he asked.

'Yes, it is still hurting,' she said.

'It will be all right in the morning,' he tried to reassure her.

He switched off the light and lay down beside her, but their bodies remained apart. Manjiri had become a woman with the inevitable pain and Ashok felt that he had not failed in his duty by losing the hardness of his pointer. Both had different thoughts in their minds as the arms of slumber embraced them both.

In the early hours of the morning when it was still dark, Manjiri woke up wanting to visit the toilet. As she put on the light, Ashok woke up as well. She visited the toilet to pass water and there she saw the damp blood stains on her sari. She saw the evidence of her passing from an innocent bride into a newly married woman. She had a cool wash and changed into a clean sari. She turned out the light and lay down beside Ashok.

'Are you all right now?' he whispered.

'Yes, after the bloody battle, I am the walking wounded.' Ashok touched her cheek and smiled. They were soon asleep.

Step Three

By January 1950, Jay Bapat had saved sufficient money and was now in a position to plan his journey to England, where he hoped to find a job and eventually make his home. Jay's wife Lata, whose natal family name was Khare, was very fond of her husband. They had grown to form an affectionate bond after their marriage two years previously in November 1947. During that time, Jay had used the rubber sheath to prevent unwanted pregnancy and now both had learned, through trial and error, the technique of sex with a missionary zeal and attained a degree of success and enjoyment. They were planning to start a family in England after Jay had got a job and a small flat for them to live in.

As a first step to their adventurous journey, Jay had completed the necessary application forms for their passports. But there were many papers he had to obtain before submitting the applications to the passport office. He had to obtain a domicile certificate from the Presidency Magistrate's office as evidence that he was an Indian national by birth and had lived in Pune. Since he had been employed for about two years he had to obtain a clearance document from the income tax office to prove that he did not owe any income tax. Thirdly he had to get a certificate from the central police station in Pune to prove that he had no criminal record. Nearly three weeks went by in getting all three documents. He was advised to take in person all the papers to the passport office, with three copies of their photographs endorsed by a notary public, along with the appropriate fee. Since the passport office was in Bombay, he had to make a day return journey to deliver all the papers in person.

'Well, Mr Bapat,' said the clerk in the passport office, 'the papers seem to be in order. Your passport will be posted to your address in Pune.'

'How long will it take for the passports to be ready?'

'About six weeks. Don't worry. Everything seems to be correct.'

Jay left the passport office and made his way to Victoria Terminus to catch the late afternoon train back to Pune. In the train a smartly dressed young man was sitting in the seat next to him.

'Hello! I am Suresh Datye,' said the stranger.

'Hello! I am Jay Bapat.'

Jay told Suresh his family background and his future plans in brief outline. Suresh listened with keen interest and after Jay had finished, he gave similar resumé of his young life. He had graduated in economics and politics from a well-known college in Pune and was planning to travel to London, where he hoped to study law and become a barrister.

'We have a lot in common,' said Jay. 'We both have a similar family background and we are both going abroad to further our careers.'

'That's true,' responded Suresh, 'but there is a difference – I am going to be a student and after qualifying I intend to return to India.'

'And you are not married,' said Jay. 'I have been married for over two years and I shall be looking for a job when I get to London. I hope to make Britain my home.'

'I don't think I would be happy to be a "foreigner" all my life,' said Suresh.

'But you would face a more virulent prejudice in Bombay after your return. Bapats and Datyes will not be welcome in the new political order. This was made abundantly clear by the dominant non-Brahmin caste in February 1948. Brahmins in general and Chitpavans in particular will be kept back through a calculated political and economic policy by the new political masters in Bombay Presidency. You will face obstacles in your legal career because you are a Chitpavan Brahmin.'

'I think you exaggerate the anti-Brahmin hatred displayed by the Maratha caste. I am sure this fear expressed by Brahmins is blown up out of all proportion. I am confident that I shall be a successful lawyer when I return to India in a few years' time.'

'I am not able to share your confidence in the future social order in Bombay Presidency. I hope you succeed. But in many towns and villages in February 1948, the dominant non-Brahmin caste clearly gave warning to us. "Brahmins get out" was the message that echoed in scores of towns and villages through thousands of house fires. I am taking that message seriously and getting out not only from Bombay Presidency but also from India,' said Jay with much conviction.

Suresh and Jay took leave of each other at Pune station and went towards their respective houses.

Three weeks after Jay had submitted his and Lata's applications for passports, Dada Bapat, Jay's father, bumped into an old friend who had been in the same class in school. This friend, called Govind Joshi, had gone to college in Bombay and taken a degree and almost immediately got a job in the port trust in Bombay, where he was an officer now. Dada asked Govind to come to his house for a meal, and Govind gladly accepted the invitation.

'Better make it a Saturday, so that you will be able to meet both my sons.'

It was the last Saturday in January when Govind came for lunch. When he arrived, Dada introduced him as his friend Govindrao Joshi. Jay and his elder brother made *namaskar* to the guest. Then Jay told him that he had made applications for passports for himself and his wife, Lata, and very soon he hoped to go to London.

'Very good news, Jay,' said Govindrao. 'Have you made any enquiries about a passage on a ship to London?'

'No, not yet,' replied Jay. 'I was going to do that after getting our passports.'

'I may be able to help in the matter. I'll make preliminary enquiries when I return to Bombay.' Govindrao Joshi took down the particulars of Jay and Lata and promised to find out about two economy class tickets for them on a ship going to London in the near future. Govindrao promised to write the details in a letter as soon as he was able to get the information.

Jay thought about the advice given by the marriage broker priest about settling abroad in order to prosper. He recalled his conversation with Suresh Datye and felt that he himself was right in trying to go to London. He thought that Suresh Datye harboured misplaced optimism about the future social conditions in Bombay. Now, out of the blue, a distant friend of his father had walked into their lives, openly approved Jay's decision to travel to London and promised positive help about the tickets on a ship to London. Jay felt confident about the future.

A month passed in this confident mood, during which Jay and Lata both tried to speak in English to each other. Sometimes they got the order of the words in a sentence wrong, and they were tempted to use long words which gave their conversation a bookish tinge. Above all they were thinking in Marathi and then translating into English.

It all sounded stiff and artificial but at least they were making a serious effort.

Towards the end of February, Jay and Lata received their passports through the post. That simple event raised their confidence a great deal. Two days later Jay received a letter from Mr Govindrao Joshi, who had made thorough enquiries and had got definite news about a ship sailing to London in July. He had written:

Dear Jay

A ship named *Jal Jawahar*, owned by the Scindia Steam Navigation Company, is scheduled to leave Bombay for London in July. They have vacancies in the economy class. Come to Bombay and I will introduce you to their booking officer. Let me know by return of post when you would be coming here so that I can contact the officer and make an appointment for you to see him. Regards to your father,

Yours, *Govindrao Joshi*

Jay and Lata felt elated. When his father read the letter he felt very happy and asked Jay to write to Govindrao the same day and plan his visit to Bombay in the middle of the following week.

Dear Govindrao Joshi,

Thank you for your letter of last week. All of us are delighted to get your help to secure economy class tickets on a ship going to London. At my father's suggestion I intend to travel to Bombay by the fast train on the morning of Wednesday next week. This will give you enough time to contact the booking officer at the Scindia Steam Navigation Company. I shall come to your office straight from the Victoria terminus station that morning.

With regards, *Jay Bapat*

He sealed the envelope and went to the post office to buy the stamps and post the letter.

When the alarm clock sounded at 4.30 a.m., Jay opened his eyes but did not leave his bed on the floor immediately because Lata was still asleep with her head on his left biceps and her left arm round his neck. He caressed her left cheek and gently tickled her behind her left ear. She awoke and instinctively pushed herself close to his body before moving away and sitting up in bed. Jay also sat up, and they smiled at each other before leaving the bed.

It was pleasantly cool in Pune in January but the weather in Bombay would be quite different that day. Jay and Lata brushed their teeth and while Lata began preparing tea, Jay lit the upright copper water heater, which burned wood. While the fire in its central chimney began to heat the water, Jay visited the toilet. The pan was countersunk in the floor and one had to squat over it, doing a balancing act. Lata had the tea ready and while they enjoyed the hot sweet drink, Jay casually mentioned that they would have to learn to use the European type of upright toilet.

'We shall have to visit some hotel either here in Pune or in Bombay to learn the English method,' remarked Lata.

'We shall do it soon,' said Jay, finishing his tea and preparing for the bathing ritual. Their bathing room had a stone floor and the walls were made waterproof with

60

cement plaster. He half filled a brass bucket with the water from the heater and carried it to the bathing room. Then he added some cold water to the water heater, which was outside the bathing room, and to the bucket to have it bearably hot. Closing the door, he poured water over himself. Then he applied soap to his head, torso, arms and legs and rubbed his body before rinsing off the lather with the remaining water. He dried himself on a soft towel, wound the damp towel round his waist and came out of the bathing room. Next he put on his vest, shirt and white cotton trousers. It was a quarter to six and it was still dark.

'I think I will take a snack lunch in Bombay, but I would like a cup of tea before I set off for Pune Station.'

While Lata was preparing to make more tea, Dada and Tai got up and came into the kitchen before busying themselves with the morning ritual of visiting the toilet and bathing. Lata made more tea for all four of them.

'Jay,' said his father, 'it would be a good idea to take two or three hundred rupees with you, in case the shipping company wants a deposit.'

Jay went to their bedroom, opened the steel trunk and took out 350 rupees. He would have to buy his ticket for the return train journey to Bombay that day. He was going to travel third class and the ticket would cost him 11 rupees. Although he was not going to need more than another 10 rupees for his lunch and bus fare in Bombay, he felt that the extra money would take care of any emergency. He drank his tea, offered *namaskar* to the deities in the family shrine and to his parents, and left their house and walked towards the nearest tonga stand. He got into the first tonga – a horse-drawn vehicle – and asked the driver to take him to the station. He arrived in good time and got his return ticket after standing in the queue for fifteen minutes. Then he went to the platform

61

where the fast train to Bombay was waiting. Surveying the third-class carriages, he boarded one where he was able to find a seat on the hard wooden bench. There were no overhead fans in the carriage, and as more passengers entered the carriage the atmosphere began to be oppressive. Everyone waited for twelve minutes before the train moved out of the station and sped towards Bombay.

Jay had done this journey many times before when he was studying at the art school in Bombay but he never failed to be surprised by the change in temperature as the train carried him from the cool and dry atmosphere of Pune towards the hot and humid air of Bombay. From Pune the train steadily climbed until it reached Lonavala, which is the highest point of the railway track. From then on, it is downhill all the way. As the train began to descend the Western Ghats, he felt the humid air of the Konkan coast surround his body and make him perspire. He had bought a newspaper at Pune station, which he now used to fan himself. As he looked around the crowded carriage he noticed that everyone was doing the same thing. Some used newspapers, some used magazines, which were more effective as make-do fans. One or two passengers had brought with them the traditional straw or palm-frond fans, which were the more effective, but of course the fans did not cool the air, they simply made the warm air move quickly about one's face, giving a feeling of some comfort in the heavy, humid atmosphere.

As the train reached Kalyan station, he noticed thick crowds on the platforms. Some early commuters pushed their way into the carriage and stood in cramped postures, holding the handrails tightly. At every station there were crowds of passengers. At Dadar many people left the train. Jay travelled on the rest of the way to Victoria Terminus. He got down on to the platform and made his way out of the grand British-built railway station and walked towards the bus stop, where he hoped to get a bus to go to the Bombay Port Trust office to meet Govindrao Joshi.

He waited in the orderly queue just outside the Victoria Terminus for maybe ten minutes before he was able to board the bus to travel to the Port Trust office. The journey was short and he paid only two annas, which was one eighth of a rupee. Within half an hour after his arrival in Bombay, he was standing at the counter at the reception desk in the office where Govind Joshi worked. Jay gave his name to the Indian Christian clerk and told him that he was there to see Mr Govind Joshi. The clerk checked the appointments list and when he noticed Jay's name on it, he sent a peon with a note to Govind Joshi.

'Hello, Jay! Welcome to Bombay,' said Govind Joshi as he came to the reception desk to escort Jay to his office. 'Take a seat, Jay. I'll phone the shipping company office and then ask the peon to get us two cups of tea.'

Jay sat in an upright wooden chair which was placed under the overhead electric fan. He heard Govind Joshi speak to Mr Patel, the booking officer at the Scindia Steam Navigation Company, and say that Jay Bapat had come from Pune and would be at the shipping company's office in time for his early afternoon appointment.

Then Govind Joshi rang the brass bell on his desk to summon the peon.

'Yes sir,' said the peon as he came into the office.

'Take this money and bring us two cups of tea from the canteen,' said Govind Joshi to the peon in his usual 'officer's tone'. The peon took the money and saying 'yes sir' again left the office.

Govind Joshi asked Jay about his father and his train journey from Pune and assured him that most probably his tickets would be confirmed that very day. As both of them enjoyed the hot sweet tea, Jay got a most welcome offer from Mr Joshi.

'Listen, Jay,' said Govind, 'you don't have any close relations living in Bombay, do you?'

'No, Mr Joshi. All our relations live in Pune or in the nearby towns.'

'I am asking you these details for a very good reason. When your date of departure is fixed, you and your wife and possibly your parents need to come to Bombay at least two days before that date. I have a spacious flat in the officers' quarters. You will all be most welcome to stay with us for at least three days.'

'That will be of great help,' replied Jay.

'Good. Your father and I were at the same school. After you leave for London, I shall be able to talk to your father about our school days.'

'Mr Joshi,' said Jay, 'can I get a snack lunch in your canteen?'

'Yes, certainly. We'll go there in a few minutes. Be my guest.'

'Thank you,' said Jay expressing his gratitude with a formal phrase.

Soon after noon, Jay went to the canteen with Mr Joshi and had a snack lunch and a cup of tea.

'I have been busy since January getting the various papers for the passports. At long last we got our passports, and now it is nearly the end of April. I may be lucky with the tickets today, thanks to you, Mr Joshi.'

Mr Govind Joshi had made an appointment, for Jay to see Mr Patel, the booking officer at the Scindia Steam Navigation Company, at three that afternoon. Since his work was nearly done, he decided to take Jay to the shipping company office and introduce him to Mr Patel in person.

'Jay,' said Govind, 'the shipping company's office is not

very far from our office, so we could take a leisurely walk and be there in good time for your appointment.'

Although Jay had trained at the art school he had never before walked in the commercial part of south Bombay known as the Fort Area. He looked in wonderment at the stone-built structures with covered pavements outside the big offices. The streets were not very crowded and were fairly clean. He noticed that there were no hawkers on the pavements and the office workers wore shirt and tie with their cotton jackets. In the centre of the wide roads from Byculla to the Gateway of India and from Girgaum to Victoria Terminus ran the inexpensive trams. The fare for a long tram ride from the 'Black Horse' – the equestrian statue of one of the British monarchs near the Gateway of India – to Kings Circle in Matunga in north Bombay, a distance of nearly twelve miles, was only two annas.

Jay noticed the 'English' street names, such as Hornby Road, Meadows Street, Flora Fountain Road and Ballard Estate, which reminded him that before India became independent in 1947, it was ruled by the British for nearly two hundred years. Soon they arrived at the office of the shipping company. Jay read the sign board *Scindia Steam Navigation Company* before he followed Govind Joshi into the building. Immediately he noticed that the air was much cooler inside. After Govind Joshi had given their names to the reception clerk and told him the purpose of their visit, he asked Jay whether he noticed anything unusual about the building.

'Yes, it is much cooler here.'

'This is one of the few air-conditioned offices in the Fort Area,' said Govind.

Mr Patel came to the reception desk.

'Hello, Mr Patel! Let me introduce my friend Mr Jay Bapat,' said Govind. 'Jay, this is Mr Patel, who will probably help you in getting a passage to London.'

Jay and Mr Patel shook hands and the two visitors followed Mr Patel into his office.

'Perhaps Mr Bapat should tell me briefly what his requirements are,' said Mr Patel.

'Well,' began Jay, 'I am a qualified draughtsman and I am married. My wife, Lata, is a housewife. We want to go to England to find employment. If we are successful, we wish to settle there and bring up a family. We want two economy class tickets on one of your passenger ships.'

'Mr Joshi had given me some idea about your proposed trip,' responded Mr Patel. 'You are in luck, because one of our ships, called *Jal Jawahar*, is due to sail for England in July and there are some vacancies in the economy class.'

'How much is the fare, Mr Patel?'

'It is 55 pounds. That comes to 715 rupees at the present rate of exchange.'

'How much deposit do I have to pay to make a firm booking?'

'You put down 100 rupees deposit for each ticket and pay the entire balance in one week.'

Jay then showed Mr Patel his and Lata's passports and counted out 200 rupees for the deposit for the tickets. Mr Patel gave Jay a receipt for the advance and told him that *Jal Jawahar* was due to sail on 17th July. Govind Joshi and Jay Bapat thanked Mr Patel for his help. As they got up from their chairs to leave, Mr Patel reminded Jay about the balance payment within one week.

Govind Joshi accompanied Jay to the Victoria Terminus station, where Jay was to catch an express train to Pune. Jay thanked him for his help and promised to keep him informed of his preparations for the voyage in July.

'Don't forget, you are to stay with us for two days before you get on the ship for London,' reminded Govind Joshi as he said goodbye. Jay had his return ticket for the journey. He made a note of the platform number for the Pune train and made his way towards it. The train was standing at the platform and Jay was able to find a seat in a third-class carriage. As he sat down he felt tired, as the tension from the day's activities was relaxed. He leant against the hard wooden seat, closed his eyes and waited. He did not wake up until the train had travelled nearly thirty miles. As he opened his eyes he saw the crowded platforms of Kalyan Junction receding in the distance. The carriage was full, with many passengers either sitting on their bags or standing wherever there was space to accommodate them.

As the train began its steady climb up the steep track towards the top of the Western Ghats, the air gradually became cooler and the oppressive humidity of Bombay remained only a memory. The humid atmosphere in the bustling city had left its marks in the sweat-stains on men's shirts. Jay's own shirt, which had been dry and clean in the morning in Pune, now looked grubby with streaks of yellow sweat-stains. When the train reached the top level of the track, most passengers relaxed and generally the carriage began to fill with animated conversations. Jay felt pleased with the day's achievement. With the help of Govind Joshi, their economy class tickets on a ship to London were booked. He was calculating the balance of fares to be paid to the shipping company when the train arrived at Pune station, after a journey lasting nearly three and a half hours. He came out of the station and found a tonga to take him home.

It was quite dark when Jay reached home. He removed his shirt and cotton trousers, draped a soft towel round his waist and had a wash in the bathing room. As he came out of the washroom, his mother told him that the evening meal would be ready in a few minutes. That was a cue for Lata to set their dinner places on the floor in the kitchen/dining room. Jay and his father sat down for their meal while Lata served the food and Jay's mother prepared jawar flour bread on the griddle. Jay told his parents and Lata all that had happened in Bombay that day.

'Dada,' said Jay, 'Mr Govind Joshi was very helpful and through him I was able to make a firm booking of our tickets to London. I have to go again to see Mr Patel at the Scindia Steam Navigation Company with the balance amount, which is 1,230 rupees.'

'When do you have to go?' asked Tai.

'Within one week,' he replied.

'Can I come with you to Bombay?' asked Lata. Jay had not considered that possibility, so he was taken aback by Lata's question.

'Jay,' said Dada, 'why don't you and Lata go to Bombay to pay the balance fare? Then Lata will be able to see the shipping company's office. Mr Patel will meet Mrs Lata Bapat as the second passenger. You could have your lunch at some restaurant in the Fort Area and return by the express train in the late afternoon.'

'I had not considered taking Lata with me,' said Jay, 'but now I will follow your suggestion and make that trip in three days' time. By the way, Mr Govind Joshi has invited all of us to stay for two days just before we embark, on *Jal Jawahar* on the 17th July.'

'That is a good idea of Govind's. I'll write him a letter to express my appreciation of his offer,' said Jay's father.

The next day Jay spent nearly two hours at his bank to withdraw the necessary cash for the balance fares as well as a hundred rupees extra for their trip to Bombay. Then he got their return railway tickets two days in advance. It was a stroke of luck that Jay managed to get the tickets reserved for railway employees to travel on the *Deccan Queen* in a special second-class carriage.

*　*　*

The second visit to Bombay was very enjoyable for Jay because Lata was with him. When they arrived at Pune station Jay told Lata that they were booked on the *Deccan Queen* train but they would be travelling in the railway servants' carriage. 'We will enjoy the luxury of fast travel to Bombay on a ticket which is priced at a little more than the third-class fare.' After they had got to their seats in the reserved carriage, the train left Pune at seven in the morning.

Lata had never travelled on the *Deccan Queen* train because all carriages except the railway servants' carriage, were for first-class ticket holders only. It was prohibitive for lower middle class people. A few minutes after leaving Pune station the train picked up speed and did not stop until it reached Lonavala station. From Lonavala the track descended until it reached Karjat station. From then on the train ran on level ground, and after stopping for three minutes at Dadar, the *Queen* arrived at the Victoria Terminus at 10.30 a.m., exactly on time.

Jay held Lata's hand as they made their way out of the crowds. Then Lata pulled her hand away but walked a few steps behind Jay until they reached the bus stop. Both got on the bus, after finding out whether it went anywhere near the Scindia Steam Navigation Company. The ride was short and they got down just outside the shipping company and entered the air-conditioned office. Jay went up to the reception desk and confidently told the clerk that he wished to see Mr Patel.

'Have you an appointment, sir?'

'No. Please inform Mr Patel that Jay and Lata Bapat are here to see him.'

The reception clerk sent a note to Mr Patel, who came out to meet them.

'Hello, Mr Bapat,' greeted Mr Patel. 'Let's go into my office.'

When inside the office, Jay introduced Mrs Lata Bapat to Mr Patel and showed him their passports.

'Well, Mr Patel,' said Jay, 'we are here to pay the balance of our economy class fare.'

Mr Patel took out his 'bookings' file. Jay counted out 1,230 rupees from his shoulder bag and put the money in front of Mr Patel. He checked the amount and made a note in the file against Jay's and Lata's names: 'economy class – paid in full'. Then he made out the official receipt and handed it to Jay.

'Well, Mr Bapat, your tickets will be ready in a week.'

'May I ask Mr Govind Joshi to collect them? As you know we live in Pune and I can't make frequent trips to Bombay.'

'Yes, a good idea,' responded Mr Patel. 'I'll contact Mr Govind Joshi when the tickets are ready. The ship *Jal Jawahar* will leave from Ballard Pier and your luggage limit is 12 cubic feet per passenger.'

'Could you give us some idea about the size of trunks we are allowed?

Mr Patel was very helpful and advised Jay and Lata that they should buy two large trunks, 3 feet by 2 feet by 1 foot, which could be kept in the hold and buy two smaller trunks, 3 feet by 1½ feet by 9 inches which could be used for cabin luggage wanted on the voyage. Mr Patel then suggested that Jay and Lata could go to the office canteen and have some tea and snacks. While sitting in the cool canteen with tea and onion fritters, Jay worked out the cubic capacity of the trunks which was well within the top limit of 12 cubic feet.

'I want to go,' whispered Lata. For a few seconds Jay did not understand the import of what Lata had said. Then it dawned on him that she wanted to visit the lavatory. Jay quietly went up to the serving counter and asked the man behind it the whereabouts of the lavatory.

'It is just outside the far door sir, separate for men and ladies,' whispered the man.

Jay told Lata in whispers where lavatory was, then busied himself in making a list of things they would have to buy for their voyage to London, while Lata left the table. He had included the four metal trunks in the list, along with various items of clothing for himself and Lata. He had read in the *Times of India* that there was rationing in England and one had to have coupons to buy even the most essential items of clothing. That was the reason why he had included clothing for both in his shopping list.

He showed the list to Lata when she came back to the table. She took a sip of her cold tea and whispered that she had had to use the 'English method' but wasn't very successful. Jay also visited the lavatory before they left the shipping company's office and went towards the Gateway of India, a famous Bombay landmark, built by the British in the early part of the twentieth century.

'Lata,' said Jay, 'when I was studying at the art school, there was a vegetarian restaurant nearby. Let's go there and have our midday meal. It was not very expensive – that was why it was popular with the students.'

'Is it very far? Do we have to take a bus?' asked Lata.

'No, it's not very far. We can walk there,' said Jay.

After nearly twenty-five minutes they found the restaurant and went in. One middle-aged waiter recognised Jay. '*Namaskar*, Mr Bapat.'

'*Namaskar*, Appaji,' Jay returned the greeting.

Jay decided to have two set meals and asked Lata whether it was all right for her. When Lata spoke her approval they ordered their lunch. Jay had been saving money to prepare to travel to London and for over two years he had not even once indulged in what he always

71

referred to as unwise spending. When they were at the Gateway of India, he had fleetingly considered having tea and biscuits at the famous Taj Mahal Hotel, but he had suppressed that thought and decided to walk to the familiar and inexpensive restaurant near the art school. They enjoyed their lunch and paid the 6 rupees bill with pleasure. They had spent 24 rupees for their return travel on the *Deccan Queen* and only 9 rupees on tea and lunch. On the spur of the moment he decided to spend another 10 rupees for a sari for Lata. As they left the restaurant, he suggested that they should take a tram to Girgaum and visit a sari shop.

'I want to buy a sari to remember this day,' he said.

Lata touched his hand in gratitude for his loving gesture. She chose a light blue cotton sari and an orange-coloured blouse piece, an eye-catching contrasting colour. Then they travelled by tram back to Victoria Terminus in good time to catch the *Deccan Queen* at 5 p.m.

The journey back to Pune was relaxing and they arrived at the station at 8.30 p.m. It was dark and cool. Dada and Tai were happy to hear that the economy class tickets to London were now firmly booked. Within three months Jay and Lata would begin their adventure of a lifetime.

By the end of May, Jay and Lata had done all their shopping. One evening Jay showed Lata a packet of twelve contraceptives which he had bought. When Lata saw them she was amused and thrilled at the same time.

'Why so many?' she asked.

'When we are on the ship we shall have a lot of time on our hands. With these "baby-stoppers" I will be able to entertain you. Besides, we are not going to start making babies until we are settled in London,' responded Jay.

Lata picked up a pencil from Jay's shoulder bag and

wrote on the packet *Wanted on Voyage*. Jay laughed loudly at the aptness of the phrase and quickly pressed his lips on her smiling mouth. Lata clung to him for a few moments to express her silent appreciation of her husband's affection.

In the second week of June Jay and Lata met Suresh Datye as they were out for a walk to the Parvati Temple on the hill.

'Hello, Suresh.'

'Hello, Jay.

'Let me introduce Lata, my wife.'

'*Namaskar*,' greeted Suresh.

'Suresh, have you got your passage booked yet?'

'Yes, but I have not paid the full fare yet. I am going to do that tomorrow.'

'What is the name of your ship?' asked Jay.

'*Jal Jawahar* of the Scindia Steam Navigation Company.'

'Really! What a coincidence. We are travelling by the same ship. But are you sure that your reservation is safe? I was given only a week to pay the balance fare, and that was towards the end of April.'

'Yes, my ticket is reserved. I had asked Mr Patel to give me longer time to pay the balance and he kindly allowed me to pay up to the middle of June. That's why I am going to Bombay tomorrow.'

Suresh went on his way back to his house after saying goodbye. Jay and Lata walked up the steps to the temple on the hill and offered silent thanks to the god Vishnu for their good fortune.

The next day a letter arrived from Bombay. It was addressed to Jay's father. When he opened it he quickly read the signature at the end of the page. It was from his school friend Govind Joshi.

Greetings and *namaskar* to Dada Bapat and family from Govind Joshi. Over a month ago I had met your

73

son, Jay, and introduced him to Mr Patel, the booking officer at the Scindia Steam Navigation Company. Jay's and Lata's tickets were confirmed on the same afternoon. I learnt from Mr Patel that Jay and Lata had called within three days and paid the balance fare. About a week later Mr Patel had phoned me to say that the tickets were ready. I was not able to pick up the tickets for another week because of pressure of work. Now I am happy to say that their economy class tickets for their voyage to London on *Jal Jawahar* are safely with me. The ship sails on 17th July. I invite you and Tai with Jay and Lata to come to Bombay and stay with me for four or five days, two days before the date of departure and two days after it. We'll be able to talk about our school days. My wife and I look forward to welcoming you all on 15th July.

That evening, after Jay had come home from the drawing office where he had been working for about two years, Dada showed him Govind Joshi's letter. After their evening meal, Dada and Tai suggested that a full day's get-together of their and Lata's family should be arranged soon. Jay pointed out that he still had to work for two more weeks before his resignation became effective, so they chose the first Sunday in July for the get-together. Jay contacted Suresh Datye and asked him to have lunch with them on that day. Dada wrote a letter to his married daughter, who lived not far from Pune, to come for the get-together with her husband and their son, and he went in person to see Lata's parents, Appa and Mai Khare, and invited them with their two unmarried daughters for the gathering. Jay's elder brother Vijay and his wife were very enthusiastic and helpful on the day. Tai Bapat and Mai Khare with their daughters cooked the food for the fourteen people present.

Suresh Datye was introduced to Appa Khare as a co-passenger on the *Jal Jawahar* with Jay and Lata. Appa made discreet enquiries through normal conversation to find out about Suresh Datye's family background and was pleased to learn that Suresh had only one younger sister and no brothers. A question arose in Appa's mind as to whether Suresh Datye would be a suitable husband for Lata's younger sister. Suresh was a Chitpavan Brahmin, so the two families would have similar social status and cultural traditions. He was going to London for his law studies and planned to return to India within three or four years. Appa was prepared to wait and hope. During the day, Appa noticed that Suresh and his second daughter had not only exchanged glances but words as well. That was a hopeful sign. Appa decided to contact his family priest and start serious enquiries about a possible marriage alliance between the Datye and Khare families.

As arranged Jay, Lata, Vijay and Tai completed the packing of the four steel trunks and Jay hired a porter to take the, heavy trunks to Pune station on the morning of fifteenth July for their travel to Bombay. The porter had got to the station before the Bapat family but he had to have another porter to help him load the heavy trunks on to the train. Dada paid both porters and boarded the train to join Tai, Jay and Lata. Vijay said goodbye to them from the platform and promised to be in Bombay with his wife to wish Jay and Lata 'bon voyage'.

The train left Pune station on time, and after nearly four hours arrived at the Victoria Terminus station in Bombay. Jay found a porter to unload the heavy trunks while Dada searched for his school friend. He saw Govind coming towards him down the platform.

'Hello, welcome to Bombay,' said Govind.

'I am glad to see you,' responded Dada. 'Now you will be able to guide us, with our luggage, to your flat.'

Govind Joshi had arranged for a porter to take the four trunks on a push cart to his flat, which was a couple of miles away. The porter was given the exact address of the flat and Jay was asked to accompany the porter on foot, while the others travelled by tram car.

It was well after midday that Jay and the porter arrived with the heavy metal trunks. When the luggage was unloaded and taken up to the first floor flat, Govind Joshi paid the porter 5 rupees. The man did not expect more than 3 rupees for his labour so he went away very happy, touching his forehead with the 5-rupee note. After lunch the hosts and guests rested. They had managed to escape the heavy downpour of the monsoons and they were relieved to be safe and dry in Govind's flat while nature was busy washing the streets and roofs of Bombay.

The next day Jay and Lata checked the contents of the four trunks and made sure that their passports and the tickets, which Govind had handed over the previous evening, were safely kept in Jay's shoulder cloth bag. The money was counted and kept in two envelopes with the passports. Govind Joshi's wife had prepared a farewell feast for the guests and the day went by in eager anticipation.

The day had at last dawned when Jay and Lata Bapat would leave India and embark on their great adventure. Vijay and his wife had decided to travel by the night passenger train, so they arrived very early at Govind's flat. Govind's wife had to prepare food for eight people for that day's lunch. All six guests got up early and busied themselves in their morning ablutions. Jay and Lata checked their luggage, passport, tickets and the cash for the third time before their early lunch. Govind had arranged to find two reliable porters with a push cart to transport the heavy trunks to the pier, and Vijay volunteered to go with them.

After lunch, Tai waved a ghee lamp before Jay and Lata to ward off evil influences, after which Govind, his wife, Dada and Tai gave their good wishes and blessings to the voyagers. All of them made their way to Ballard Pier. Jay and Lata checked with the embarkation officer, who told them that their luggage was already on the ship. After a tear-filled goodbye, Jay and Lata boarded *Jal Jawahar*. They quickly walked up the gangway and stood behind the railings to wave at the relatives who stood on the pier looking up and trying to focus on them. At this point Suresh Datye joined Jay and Lata and began waving a handkerchief towards his relatives who were standing in the crowd on the pier. All visitors were asked to leave the ship.

Within twenty minutes the ship's engines came to life and the *Jal Jawahar* slowly pulled away from the pier. The passengers continued to wave their handkerchiefs until Bombay harbour was a vague outline and the people on the pier appeared to be tiny dots. Jay and Lata dried their tears and made their way towards the economy class cabins.

Their cabin, No. 63, was on the lower deck, where there was an open area at the back and in the centre of the ship. They were lucky to have a small cabin for two passengers, with twin beds and a wash basin. Their cabin trunks were placed under the porthole next to a cupboard for clothes. There was a table, and two chairs; Jay noticed that the furniture legs were fastened to the wooden floor with short chains. The bathroom with a tub was next to the four lavatories which were for the economy class passengers.

After freshening up they found the dining room for their section. A steward greeted them.

'Good afternoon, sir, good afternoon, madam. What is your cabin number please?'

'Sixty-three.'

'Yes, here it is,' he said, checking a list pinned on the dining room door. 'Mr and Mrs Bapat.' (Actually the Goan steward said 'Mr and Mrs Baypaat.')

'The name is Baapat,' said Jay.

'I am George. Your cabin steward is Peter, and your table number is twelve. Four other passengers will be at your table.'

'Thank you, George,' said Jay as they went up on the deck in the middle of the ship. They walked unsteadily towards the railings and looked at the green and frothy expanse of the Arabian Sea.

Many other passengers came on the deck in ones and twos, all holding on to the railings and looking at the greenish water around them. Although they all felt the vibrations underfoot, there was no obvious sense of forward movement, yet they knew that the ship was moving westwards towards the African coast.

Suresh Datye met them on the deck and gave them some useful information.

'Hello! I've been reading the notices near the dining room door. Breakfast will be at 8.30 a.m., lunch at 1.00 p.m., afternoon tea at 4.00 p.m. and the evening meal at 7.30 p.m. There is a café/bar where we can get tea, coffee, beer or fruit juice and pay for the drinks either in rupees or English money. The four main meals are included in the price of our tickets. My cabin is twenty-nine, which I share with two other passengers, both of them men.'

'What is your table number in the dining room?'

'It is twelve,' replied Suresh.

'We are also at number twelve,' said Lata.

'Have you met any Marathi speakers?' asked Jay.

'No, not in person, but I read some Marathi names on the notice board near the dining room.'

They wandered on the lower and middle decks, where the economy class cabins were situated, and noticed that the cabin numbers ran from 51 to 100. The first-class cabins, numbered 1 to 50, were situated on the lower and the middle decks in the front part of the ship. There was a large square space on the lower deck between the first and economy class cabins. They could not imagine its purpose. Then they overheard snatches of conversation between an Anglo-Indian couple and their teenage son who were also travelling economy class, going 'home' to the UK.

'Look, Dad, that's where they are going to set up the canvas swimming pool.'

'How do you know, son?' asked the father.

'The ship's purser told me.'

As they made their way to the dining room, other passengers also converged on the 'eating place'. It was fairly large and could easily accommodate all the economy class passengers. Jay, Lata and Suresh met the other three passengers who were going to eat at table No. 12. One was a law student from Bombay named Arvind and the other two were Amer and Meera Chatterjee from Calcutta, who spoke Bangali but understood Marathi, since they had lived in Bombay for the previous two years. Tea, cakes and biscuits were served by the dining room steward. Jay and Suresh told the steward that they were vegetarians, and Arvind said he was half vegetarian since he ate eggs and fish and not meat. Amer and Meera also did not eat red meat but were quite happy with fish and eggs. The steward informed them that there would be rice and vegetable curry every evening, so the vegetarians would not starve. After tea Jay and Lata stayed in their cabin, sorting out clothes and other belongings which would be needed for the voyage.

After the evening meal on the first day they returned to their cabin. Closing the door behind him, Jay embraced Lata and kissed her deeply, his hands encircling her and gradually resting on her plump behind. He pulled her towards him, which brought their crotches against each other, causing a slight surge of desire through that firm and close contact. Lata gently stroked his back and pushed her lower body against his, thus indicating without words that she wanted naked physical contact. Jay suggested that they should partially undress, baring their lower bodies, and lie down on one of the single beds, after visiting the toilet to empty their bladders. They left off their underpants and lay side by side in very close bodily contact, lightly kissing and touching.

'I can feel the throbbing of the ship's engines on this bed. When we were standing or sitting we did not notice that gentle vibration,' whispered Lata.

'Let me get in between your thighs,' whispered Jay, 'then you will feel the urgent throbbing of my engine.'

Lata gave out a suppressed laugh at his joke as Jay positioned himself for his missionary pleasure. Then suddenly he got up from the bed and opened one of the rubber 'baby-stoppers' which he had kept ready on the table. He crawled back into position, fitted the 'stopper' and eagerly moored his engine in Lata's harbour. Lata felt the familiar rubber-coated friend filling her harbour to capacity. Instinct guided her pelvis to move up and down to meet Jay's strong movements. Jay put his engine in the overdrive and made Lata tremble with pleasure before emptying his energy into the rubber baby-stopper.

Their first night on the ship was restful, but the morning of the second day brought them an uneasy queasy feeling in the stomach due to the oppressive oily smell in the cabin and the steady vibrations of the ship's diesel engines which seemed to shake the whole ship. Jay got out of bed first and visited the toilet. There was nobody about although it was well past breakfast time. As he walked unsteadily to their cabin he found Lata standing near the wash basin and making retching sounds although she did not vomit. He also got a feeling of nausea and moved towards the wash basin. He experienced strong retching but the contents of his stomach did not gush out. Both felt a slight headache and instinct made them lie on their beds. In that supine position the feeling of sickness slightly subsided. They brushed their teeth and washed, still with that nausea, and felt that a cup of tea would bring them relief.

When they entered the dining room they found it almost empty. Only six or eight people were having breakfast. The steward brought their tea. The hot drink gave a feeling of comfort in the stomach. They did not eat anything. As soon as they went on the deck they rushed to the railings and both emptied the contents of their stomachs over the side of the ship. It was their first ever experience of sickness. After vomiting they somehow made their way back to their cabin and washed their mouths and splashed their faces with cold water.

'I brought some cloves,' said Lata, 'but I can't remember where I put them.'

'I don't think cloves would be much use,' said Jay. 'What we need...' He did not finish the sentence. He was bending over the wash basin, retching. Lata lay down on the bed and shut her eyes. The ship was far away from land and totally at the mercy of the sea. It had begun to rise and dip along the direction of the journey and Lata felt that rising and dipping motion. With each rise and fall her stomach was affected. Now Jay lay on the bed and also experienced a sinking feeling with the pitching motion of the sea. Both of them must have dozed off for over an hour. When they woke up, Jay heard knocking on the cabin door. He staggered to the door and opened it to find Suresh Datye standing and beaming with health.

'Hello, Jay,' he said. 'How are you?'

'We both are seasick,' replied Lata from her bed.

'I have some tablets for seasickness. I'll go and get them from my cabin,' said Suresh.

'Look, I have four tablets for you,' he said when he came back. 'Take one now and one after lunch. You are not advised to take more than two each day.'

'Thank you, Suresh,' said Jay and Lata at the same time.

They took a tablet each and kept the other two for later.

'How is it, Suresh, that you are not seasick?'

'Just lucky today. Can't say what will happen tomorrow.'

'Is there anywhere on the ship where we can buy these tablets?' asked Lata.

'I don't know. Perhaps we could ask the purser later on.'

After their vomiting Jay and Lata did not want to eat anything and said so to Suresh, who did not agree. 'Have some dry biscuits or bread, that will help, I am sure.'

He suggested that they should go on the top deck on the economy class side of the ship and see the sea view from that vantage point. Jay and Lata were not very enthusiastic at first but after a little persuasion they agreed to accompany Suresh. There were only two people on the top deck who had come there to find out more about their surroundings. The cabins were only on the lower and middle decks. The top deck was a substantial area set aside for deck games, for people to relax in deck chairs and to serve as an assembly point for the lifeboat drill.

On one wall of the staircase enclosure, Lata noticed about forty rope rings of six-inch diameter, hung on half dozen pegs, and instructions about a game called deck quoits. When this game is played on land, the players stand a fixed distance away and throw the rings to encircle the pegs on the ground. But this was adapted to be played on a ship. Instead of pegs on the ground, there were three concentric circles painted on the deck in three places, so that three different teams could play the game at the same time. Standing on the starting line, a player had to throw the quoits to land them near or on the innermost circle to score maximum points. It appeared to be an easy game but there was nothing on the deck to stop the quoits from skidding away from the circles. The players had to judge the distance and the speed of the throw to achieve success. Lata persuaded Jay and Suresh to try the game. They soon realised that it was not as easy as it looked. They looked at the ten lifeboats on their part of the ship and found that they were sufficient for the 120 economy class passengers. They assumed that there were similar lifeboats on the top deck of the first-class section at the front of the ship.

The time spent on the top deck made Jay and Lata forget their seasickness for some time. Fresh sea air did not cause the same discomfort as the cabin atmosphere had done. All three went to the dining room when lunch time came. Suresh was quite happy to order vegetable curry and rice, but Jay and Lata asked for plain bread.

'Can I make you some toast?' asked the steward. 'It will help to fight the seasickness.'

One hour after lunch, both Jay and Lata were sick. The dry toast did not help. They contacted the purser, who advised them to buy tablets from the ship's shop. They now took the second tablet which Suresh had given them and bought a packet of twenty more. They decided to skip the evening meal and retire to their cabin and rest. The first day of their voyage had brought them varied experiences.

*   *   *

Jay and Lata suffered from seasickness for four days with
much vomiting, and Suresh was also seasick for two days.
On the fifth day of the voyage, their stomachs settled and
they began to enjoy their food and looked forward to the
meal times eagerly.

The ship ploughed the Arabian Sea with a rhythmic
pitching motion, but the passengers now hardly noticed
the ship's motion or the vibrations of the engines. Jay
and Lata played the deck game with other passengers or
rested in the deck chairs or sometimes played cards. When
they stood at the railings on the top deck they could see
the vast expanse of green water and the curve of the
horizon in the distance. There was a white foam trail in
the ship's wake. They also took part in the 'distance
guessing' each day. In the beginning their guess was way
off the correct number, but after working out the speed
of the ship, they were able to get close to the actual
number of nautical miles that the ship had travelled.

Early in the morning on the fifth day they went past
the island of Socotra in the Gulf of Aden, and the next
day the ship docked in Aden harbour. Aden was a British
possession but passengers were not able to go on land
because the ship was halting there for only six hours.

'Jay, have you read much British period history of India?'
asked Suresh.

'Only what was dished out in the high school text books,'
replied Jay.

'In 1857, the Indian uprising was put down by the
British but Indians continued their struggle right up to
1947. In 1875, Vasudev Phadkay organised a band of
Ramoshee men to rise against the British administration
in western India but his effort was defeated and Phadkay
was deported to Aden jail. In 1906 another patriot, named

Vinayak Savarkar, travelled along this route on his way to England. He was a free man then, but within five years his life changed and he carried on the Indian independence struggle single-handed and in an unconventional manner,' said Suresh.

'Sureseh, you mentioned Phadkay and Savarkar,' said Jay, 'but there were many other Chitpavan Brahmins who made a great sacrifice and took part in the independence struggle in many fields. But Independent India seems to have forgotten the Chitpavan contribution. That's why Lata and I are leaving India to settle in England.'

After the ship left Aden, the air temperature became high as the *Jal Jawahar* entered the Red Sea, which had deserts on both banks. The water was no longer a pleasing green but a reddish muddy colour.

It had taken the ship six days to travel from Bombay to Aden and after two more days in the Red Sea, they arrived at Suez, which was also a British-controlled town, at the entrance to the Suez Canal. At Suez a specialist navigator, called the pilot, took control of the ship and piloted it through the canal until they reached Port Said.

It had taken them nine days to reach Port Said, and although the weather was hot, Jay, Lata and Suresh had begun to enjoy their voyage. They no longer suffered any seasickness and had made friends with some Marathi-speaking passengers. Raja and Arvind (their table companions) came from Bombay and were law students hoping to become barristers. Vinu was an accountant in his late twenties and was married to Suman, who was a stenographer/typist. Suresh Datye got on well with the two law students.

Britain had her Indian Empire for nearly two hundred years, and, after the Suez Canal was constructed, the

British controlled not only the entire canal zone but the various points of strategic importance such as Aden, Cyprus, Malta and Gibraltar. These were firmly held by the British in order to protect the route from Britain to India through the canal. In the early years of the East India Company, communications between London and Calcutta were very slow since the sailing ships had to travel round the southern tip of Africa. After the Suez Canal construction, the journey time was shortened and the age of steam had arrived, thus helping both the trade with the East as well as the security of the RaJ because men and materials could be transported to India relatively quickly.

When the ship reached Port Said, a short trip was arranged to enable some passengers to visit the Pyramids near Cairo, the capital of Egypt. Nearly all the first-class passengers and only twenty from economy class took advantage of the trip. Jay and Lata decided not to spend their hard-saved money on these extras at this point of their adventure. Some time in the future after they were well settled in Britain, they could make a special effort to see the Pyramids.

Jay had looked up the distance between various towns on the route. Cairo was nearly 2,700 miles from Bombay and the distance between Bombay and London was almost 4,500 miles by the Mediterranean route.

The pilot handed over the controls to the company captain and, after the passengers who had gone to see the Pyramids returned to Port Said, *Jal Jawahar* slowly left the port and entered the shipping channel in the Mediterranean to travel west.

Jay and Lata noticed the change in atmospheric temperature. It was no longer oppressively hot and sultry but pleasantly cool during the day and a little chilly at night.

'Do you remember the colour of the Arabian Sea?' asked Jay.

'Yes,' said Lata, 'it was definitely green.'

'All that water in the Arabian Sea was joined to the Red Sea,' continued Jay, 'but that did not change the colour of the smaller sea. It remained muddy red.'

'That's right,' responded Lata, 'the water in the canal itself was oily grey but now the water in the Mediterranean Sea is light blue.'

As they talked about the colours of the various seas, they were looking at the map of the southern part of Europe. The island of Crete appeared to be larger than Malta. They also noticed the words *Malta Channel* and *Sicilian Channel*. The ship was to follow those channels en route to Gibraltar. They had read on the notice board that the ship would sail past Malta on the second night after leaving Port Said, and they stood on the deck for nearly half an hour hoping to see the distant lights of the island. The weather was very cool so they stood very close, with arms around each other to keep warm. There were two other couples standing further away also trying to glimpse the lights. The ship pitched gently in the calmer sea. The cool of the night and the close contact with each other's bodies brought a deep romantic feeling to Jay and Lata. After looking at the distant lights of Malta, Jay kissed Lata in the dark and indicated with a close embrace his desire to have close intimacy with her. Lata was thrilled at the prospect as they slowly made their way back to their cabin.

As soon as the cabin door was locked Lata, most unexpectedly for Jay, took the lead and began to remove Jay's clothes, telling him in whispers that he should return the compliment. Both found the task very exciting and as they shed their clothes their inhibitions also went with the garments. Lata was behaving very freely. She decided

87

to fit the baby-stopper on Jay's pointer, which very nearly caused Jay to lose control. However, with determination he let her complete the operation and made her lie on the bed, then kneeling between her spread thighs, he pushed his pointer in her secret fold with much vigour. As soon as she had trapped the pointer in her opening, she set up a gentle rhythm which complemented Jay's in and out movements. Because of the mutuality of their desires they experienced the culmination at the same time, which had not happened before. This new sensation brought them emotionally close and both felt the beginnings of a deeper bond between them. They had slowly and imperceptibly begun to fall in love with each other. A not very common phenomenon in an arranged marriage.

Three days passed after the lights of Malta brought Lata and Jay their unique experience. Both were enjoying their freedom and adventure. The sea air and totally new environment had affected them both. It was as if some magical power had brought them closer to each other and enlivened their physical desire for each other.

On the fifteenth day of the voyage the seven Marathi-speaking passengers in the economy class gathered in the lounge after the evening meal. Suresh suggested that they could play cards. Raja, Vinu and Arvind made a foursome for bridge. Then Suman wanted to join in, so the five of them started a different game. Jay and Lata stayed in the lounge for a while, but Lata was anxious to go back to their cabin. Jay noticed her mood and quietly they slipped out of the lounge and went to their cabin.

'Jay, I don't know why but my body feels hungry for you,' she said, removing her pants.

'Lata, I feel the same. I think it is the sea air and the carefree life on the ship.'

'Sometime tomorrow, the ship will sail past the Rock of Gibraltar but I want to meet our own Rock of Gibraltar this evening,' said Lata.

After they had emptied their bladders, Jay put on the baby-stopper and introduced his Rock of Gibraltar into Lata's strait. After a few minutes, reversing the roles, Lata managed to climb on the rock to experience a totally new sensation. The lovers slept the Sleep of Satisfaction after Jay's rock had soothed Lata's strait for a long time.

During the night *Jal Jawahar* indeed sailed through the Straits of Gibraltar and entered the more turbulent waters of the eastern Atlantic and began her north-bound journey along the coast of Portugal.

The atmosphere was decidedly chilly now and the passengers had to wear warm clothing. The pitching of the ship increased and when the ship entered the Bay of Biscay many passengers became seasick for a couple of days. Now the passengers experienced the European climate with a little dampness in the air. The English Channel was equally rough but everyone knew that the journey's end was near and gladly put up with the heavy pitching of the ship.

In the early hours of the twenty-first day of the voyage, *Jal Jawahar* neared the docks at Tilbury and as the grey dawn broke over England, the ship's engines stopped and everyone felt the stillness. The carefree days were over. Jay and Lata, along with many others, prepared to disembark and step into a new life of material shortages, rationing, a totally new and sometimes bewildering lifestyle and a cold and damp climate. They had embarked upon this adventure to settle in a strange land where social, material and professional struggles awaited them.

Arvind had obtained an address in north London where

rooms with cooking facilities could be rented. Jay and Lata decided to accompany him to the house and possibly rent a double room. After disembarking, all passengers were directed towards a large Customs shed where their luggage was going to be brought after it was unloaded from the ship. Everyone was assured that the luggage would be placed in alphabetical order. Jay, Lata and Arvind waited patiently outside the shed. When the luggage was arranged as announced, Jay and Lata stood by their trunks. After they had informed the Customs officer of the contents of the trunks, their luggage was cleared and they were free to take it to the boat train. Jay got a porter to help with the luggage, for two shillings, bought two tickets to London and boarded the train. Arvind had managed to join them with his one trunk.

It was a grey morning with a steady drizzle, which was to be expected in early August. The train left Tilbury station and after fifty minutes' journey steamed into St Pancras station belching out smoke and soot. Jay and Arvind managed to get a taxi and load the luggage on to it and the three of them reached the address near Swiss Cottage station. The taxi cost them a pound. When Jay rang the bell, the door was opened by an English woman.

'Hello, we have just, larrived from Bombay looking for somewhere to stay.'

'Come in,' said the woman. 'This is Mr Gupta, my husband, I am Mary.'

Jay and Lata managed to rent a double room for £3 10s per week with cooking facilities, while Arvind got a single room for £2 per week.

Mr Gupta and Arvind helped with the luggage and when all the trunks were brought into the two rooms, Mary asked the new arrivals into their sitting room, on the ground floor, for a cup of tea, and she explained the layout of the house.

'Jay and Lata,' began Mary, 'your room has a two-ring gas cooker, a sink with hot and cold water, a table and two chairs, a double bed, a bedside lamp, and a small sofa. I shall provide bed linen, which you will have to wash regularly. You can send the bed sheet and pillow cases to the laundry, which is not very expensive.'

'How do we light the gas fire in the room?' asked Lata.

'There is a gas meter which takes shilling coins, and one shilling will last for about two hours.'

'How many people live in the house?' asked Arvind.

'Myself and Ben Gupta – by the way, his name is Baniprasad, but everyone calls him Ben. There are two students who live on the top floor. And you three. There are two toilets and one bathroom. Please use paper in the toilet. There is a water heater in the bathroom. It is operated by penny coins. Usually four or five pence are sufficient for a "bucket and bowl" bath. You must keep the bathroom floor dry.'

'We shall need to buy milk, sugar, tea, bread and some vegetables. Is there a shop nearby?' asked Jay.

'Yes, the shop is quite near and as it closes at five thirty, you had better do the shopping soon.'

After tea and useful information from Ben and Mary, Jay and Lata went back to their room and looked for the teapot, kettle, pots and pans, crockery and cutlery. Mary and Ben had made them welcome and Lata noticed that there were sufficient utensils in the room. The electric light was included in the rent but they had to use shilling coins to operate the gas meter for cooking as well as heating the room.

Jay took out three pounds from the trunk and he and Lata went out to do some shopping. The rain had stopped. The streets were clean and quiet, the cars and buses were driven with much discipline and there were official crossings for people on foot. They followed the directions given to them by Ben and found the small family shop which was run by the Johnsons. As they walked into the shop, Mr Johnson said with a smile, 'Hello! Are you new here?'

'Yes we came this morning from Bombay.'

'Welcome to London!' said Mr Johnson. 'You can buy everything that you will need here, but some items are rationed. So give me your name, age and address and I shall register your names with the Council Office and get your ration cards and clothing coupons.'

'When will that be?'

'In two or three days. Tell me what you need today and I'll get it for you.' Mr Johnson was very helpful. Jay and Lata realised that they would need to make a shopping list. That day, their first in England, they bought from the shop, milk, bread, biscuits, potatoes, carrots, salt, cornflakes and small cakes. Mr Johnson agreed to let them have some tea and sugar but they would have two weeks crossed off from their ration cards when they got them later in the week. They also realised that they would have to bring a shopping bag in the future. Mr Johnson gave them a paper carrier bag to carry their goods and charged them threepence for it. Their food and vegetables would last them three or four days and the total cost of the first day's shopping was eighteen shillings.

As they came back, Mary opened the door and gave them two keys, one for the front door and one for their room. Arvind came down and was going to get some food from the shop. Lata made some tea in a teapot, which was a totally new experience. She had brought some home-ground spices from Bombay, so she was able to make a tasty vegetable curry that evening. They ate the curry with bread for their first meal in their own room.

Jay and Lata discussed various matters about their day-to-day living. Some items could be sent to the laundry but other items of clothing would have to be washed in the sink in the room and dried on the clothes line in the back garden. Gradually, during that first week, Jay and Lata learned how to use paper in the toilet, the water heater in the bathroom, and the gas meter and gas fire, which they needed to light for some time in the evenings. They got their ration cards from the Johnsons and also bought a shopping bag, soap, soap powder and a further supply of food, including some long-grain American rice. Lata found that it was impossible to buy yoghurt. Nobody knew what the item in question looked like.

Ben Gupta and his wife Mary were very helpful and advised Jay and Lata about bus routes, underground railway travel, the local library and the nearest cinema. Jay managed to get help from the local library about finding jobs for himself and Lata. They had to learn to speak quietly and use 'please' and 'thank you' for over fifty times a day. They found it difficult to speak English readily for they were thinking in Marathi, their mother tongue, and translating their thoughts into English. The expressions were not quite 'English' and their Indian accent was a handicap.

After two weeks in England, Jay calculated that they would have to spend at least £7 per week for the basic minimum food and comfort. He had with him about £150, so he and Lata would have to find jobs soon if he was to save at least £100 from his nest egg. They decided to visit the library each day and look through the newspapers for job vacancies. Getting jobs was now the top priority for them both.

The English summer was nearly over. Soon they would have to buy coats, woollen sweaters, woollen gloves and umbrellas. Jay's shoes were practically new but Lata would have to buy waterproof yet fashionable shoes so that she could wear socks to keep her feet warm in the winter. They got advice from Mary Gupta about how to maximise the clothing coupons and buy adequate winter garments.

They discussed the matter and decided to buy the clothes after getting employment.

Towards the end of August, after they had been in London for just over three weeks, Jay came across a very promising advertisement for a job in a drawing office. He wrote down the name of the firm of architects, the address and phone number and the nature of the job. The wages were slightly above average.

He got advice from Ben about travelling by the underground and about his clothes and appearance. He wrote a formal application for the job, giving full details about his qualifications, experience in Bombay and his marital status.

'Lata,' he said, when the application was ready, 'I think I'll take the application in person. That way I will be able to see the office and also note the time taken for the journey.'

'Can I come with you?' asked Lata.

'Yes, of course,' he responded.

They walked to the underground station, bought return tickets and travelled to Baker Street. Jay found the address of the firm. He walked into the building and handed his application to the receptionist. 'Thank you, Mr Baypat,' said the girl.

'It is sounded Baapat. The first "a" is long and the second "a" is short.'

'Baapat ... Baapat ... it is quite easy really,' said the receptionist.

'Yes it is.'

'Can you wait for a minute? I'll take the letter to the Manager.' Jay and Lata were pleased that the application was in the right office. The girl informed Jay that the Manager would get in touch in a week. They walked back to the station and made the return journey without much difficulty.

One week later Jay received a letter in reply to his application. He looked at the letter heading – *Brown, Wood, Steel and Company, Architects.*

Jay was to attend a formal interview two days later. He was asked to be at the Baker Street office by mid-morning. He took with him his certificate with the final examination result which had given him his technical qualification as a draughtsman. There were three candidates at the interview, but they were after another job. Jay was very lucky because his qualification was better than that of the only other candidate for his job. He was to work in the company's Waterloo office, which was also lucky, because Jay could travel on the same underground railway line from Swiss Cottage station.

'Hello,' said Lata, as Jay returned home.

'Hello, I got the job,' he told her, and gave the details of the office where he was to work and, importantly, he told Lata that his weekly wage would be £8 10s.

Lata was very happy to hear all the news and to express her happiness she kissed him and indicated that they should mark the event by using a baby-stopper. After a tasty meal they retired early and celebrated Jay's success in getting a job.

When Jay started his job, Lata spent some time in the local library every afternoon. After about a month she managed to get a job as a filing clerk in an estate agent's office in the same area of north London. She was quite happy to get £6 10s per week.

Their joint income was now £15 so, after getting advice from Mary Gupta, Jay and Lata bought clothes to keep them warm in the winter. They managed to live tidily in their double room and establish friendly relations with the Guptas and the various local shops.

Jay and Lata had been writing regular letters to their family in Pune and the latest letter from Jay's father brought news of the satisfaction which the family felt at Jay's and Lata's progress in their new country.

Britain was gradually overcoming the damage caused by the Second World War and there were opportunities for jobs in various fields. In 1950 many people came to London from the West Indies to work. This was done at the invitation of the government because white British people were not willing to do certain jobs, such as the transport industry and the night shifts in the cotton and woollen mills of the North of England.

Soon Jay and Lata established their place in the workforce and made steady progress. It was in July 1951 that Lata had a lucky break. She came across an advertisement for an unfurnished flat to let, through the estate agent's office where she worked. She had a word with the manager and indicated that she and her husband would like to take the flat with the controlled rent. The manager was very helpful in making arrangements and supervising the legal paperwork so that Jay and Lata could indeed get the flat at a very reasonable rent of £15 7s per calendar month.

The flat had two bedrooms and a living room, with gas fires. The kitchen was large enough to be used as a dining room as well. The toilet was separate from the bathroom. There were three other similar flats in the house, one of which was occupied by the Polish landlord and his English wife. The other two flats were rented by middle-class English couples. Jay and Lata decided to furnish one bedroom and the living room, and bought the essential items of furniture and kitchen utensils. The kitchen sink was large, so Lata was able to wash some clothes and use the clothes line in the back garden, along with other tenants. The new flat was near Finchley Road underground station, which was on the same line for Jay

96

to travel to work, and Lata's place of work was within walking distance.

Thus it was that Jay and Lata had moved into their own flat by September 1951.

Step Four

The second of February 1952 was indeed a day to remember for Ashok and his wife Manjiri.

Following their marriage in April 1950, Baba Joshi had performed the important ceremony of welcoming his daughter-in-law into their home at Wai. After spending a few days at Wai, Ashok and Manjiri went to Satara, a distance of twenty miles, so that Ashok could resume his job and Manjiri could set up their home at Satara. Although Satara was a city of different characteristics from Sangli, where Manjiri was born and educated, she was quite at home there for two reasons. Firstly, there was no language difficulty since Marathi was the main language of communication both at Sangli and Satara. Secondly, she and Ashok had begun to enjoy each other's bodily warmth in bed.

She remembered her wedding night. After they had got to their room that night, Ashok had manfully fulfilled his duty and removed her innocence, causing her much pain and drawing blood in his tearing hurry. She remembered her words when Ashok had asked her if she was all right. 'Yes, after the bloody battle, I am the walking wounded.' After nearly twenty-one months of practice she was quite hale and hearty and looked forward to each encounter with eager anticipation. Manju had made a pleasant home for the two of them and, now, had fallen in love with Ashok. They had begun saving money for their future emigration to London, but that was nearly six years away.

Ashok had learnt to work hard and do his work efficiently, gaining valuable management experience as an assistant at the ST Depot. He had rented a house which was spacious, with a small courtyard at the front, four rooms on the ground floor and three rooms on the first floor. There was a dimly lit room between the sitting room and the kitchen on the ground floor. The fourth room at the back had a stone-floored bathing area which was partitioned off from the wood fuel stove used to heat the water. Since the floor was paved with black stones, one could splash water without causing any damage.

The lavatory at the front was old-fashioned: the night soil was collected in a basket and removed each morning by a team of low-caste men employed by the municipality. That aspect of Indian society was not questioned by the high-caste people who had condemned a whole section of society to doing this dirty and degrading work for life. The Indian mind had not considered the use of machines for such dirty work because machines would bring un-employment to the night-soil removers. Soon after the Independence in 1947, the government was concentrating on industrialisation to bring India into the twentieth century. Mahatma Gandhi had pointed out this 'injustice' inflicted by 'civilised' Indians on a whole caste throughout India, but machines had not replaced the manpower engaged in this life sentence. Of course the big cities had underground sewers and flush lavatories, but in thousands of towns and villages there was no concept of public hygiene and sanitation. Those in 'Society' kept themselves clean and expected the 'unclean' caste men and women to clean up after them. So Ashok and Manju made the best of the facilities available without even thinking about the lack of public hygiene at Satara. They were only concerned about planning to go and settle in London. They had discussed the matter of children and decided to make one baby.

Raj was a healthy, handsome and very talented college student in 1950, in his final year studying for a BA degree in Marathi at the New College at Pune. He had grey-green eyes and a very light complexion, and from his physical characteristics it was clear that he was born and brought up in a Chitpavan Brahmin family in Pune. Both his parents were endowed with similar physical attributes and both were teachers in Pune. The father taught at a boys' secondary school. Raj was an only child, much loved by his parents. Since there were no siblings in the family, Raj did not have to fight for his share of food and clothing, as often happened in large families where a lower middle class father had to feed and clothe six or seven children on a limited income.

He wore good-quality clothes throughout his primary and secondary school days, and when he joined the college he always appeared in white shirt, white trousers and open sandals. His clothes were well washed and ironed. His father had bought him a bicycle as an 'encouragement' gift for passing the matriculation examination. Of course, in Pune owning a bicycle was quite normal because hundreds of people used it as a routine independent means of transport. Another reason was the nature of the terrain on which Pune had been built. There were no steep hills and dales there. The roads were level and there were very few private cars. There was a bus service but most people – men and some young women – preferred the bicycle since it gave the rider freedom and independence.

Maya was very beautiful and clever. She had light

complexion and green eyes, for she was the eldest of three daughters of a Chitpavan Brahmin judge who was noted for his simple lifestyle and stern attitude to impartial justice. He was financially well off, with his own house in a fashionable ward in the middle of the Chitpavan stronghold called Sadashiv Peth, an area named after a brave and astute cousin of the Brahmin Peshwa of Pune. The Peshwas were the ministers of the Maratha Kings who ruled at Satara and the de facto rulers of the Maratha Confederacy, although the King was the nominal head of State.

Maya was born with a silver spoon in her mouth, lived in a loving environment, enjoyed the comforts of an upper middle class Hindu family and studied at the same college as Raj. She was also in the final year, preparing for a BA degree in Marathi.

In the second year of their BA course when there was hardly any examination pressure and stress, both Raj and Maya took an enthusiastic part in the annual social gathering of the college and displayed their flair for acting in a romantic comedy, in which they were cast as the two leads. During the course of rehearsals and the final two performances of the play they fell in love with each other and took every opportunity to be with each other. When the college classes finished in the afternoon, Raj and Maya often went to an Iranian tea shop, run by a Parsee family, where they would sit opposite each other drinking their flavoured tea, gazing into each other's eyes and, on occasions, holding hands across the table as an affectionate gesture. Raj could not imagine his future life without Maya, and Maya loved him with equal intensity.

One day Raj asked Maya to go for an early evening stroll with him. She eagerly accepted the invitation and agreed to meet him at the entrance to their college. When she saw Raj with his bicycle she was quite puzzled.

'Why do you need your bicycle when we are supposed to go for a leisurely stroll?'

'This is a kind of insurance. If you get tired of walking I can give you a lift on the crossbar.'

This daring hint intrigued Maya but she did not immediately respond. Raj wheeled his bicycle, holding the handlebar with his right hand, and as Maya walked on his left, he was able to hold her right hand with a caressingly loose contact. The touch thrilled Maya as they walked rather absent-mindedly towards the Parvati Temple just outside and to the south of Pune city. They thought of climbing the wide paved steps to the temple on the hill but decided against it because Raj did not wish to leave his bicycle unattended. He did not have the chain and padlock with him and he was not inclined to push the machine up the hundred or so steps.

'Let's sit here,' he said, pointing to some stone steps at the bottom of the hill. Maya silently agreed. After putting his bicycle at a close distance, Raj came to sit next to her on the steps, and Maya moved very close to him until their shoulders and legs were in physical contact. There were many people who were either coming down the hill or preparing to climb the steps, so Raj and Maya had no privacy in that public place. However, in half an hour or so, they were alone sitting on the bottom step, holding hands.

'We shall have to study hard for our BA finals next year,' said Maya.

'Yes, next year at college will be very busy.'

'What are you going to do after the BA?' asked Maya.

'I don't know yet ... but I would...'

'Why do you stop, Raj?'

He heard Maya's question but remained silent, deeply lost in his innermost thoughts – marriage to Maya, getting engaged before that, meeting Maya's parents, especially her father, his love for Maya... He did not give voice to any of these innermost thoughts.

When Maya repeated her question he softly whispered in her ear, 'I would like to kiss your lips.' She was thrilled to hear her own inner thoughts expressed by Raj and slowly turned her head and brought her lips close to his mouth. Cautiously he moved his mouth to contact her lips. Their lips were now softly pressed against each other. A strange new sensation surged through Maya's body. She slightly turned her upper body and pressed close to Raj's chest. Her sleepy nipples and budding breasts encased in a thin cotton bra felt the hardness and also the heat coming from Raj's chest. Raj put his right hand around Maya's shoulder and gently pulled her to him. Their breathing and heart beat quickened but their mouths remained closed. After five minutes Maya pulled her mouth away from his but remained in close contact with his body.

'Would you like to come to my house tomorrow morning, Raj, so that we can walk together to the college?'

'Yes, that would be nice.'

They moved away from each other and got up. There was no one about now. The street lights glowed silently.

'Can I try sitting on the crossbar?' asked Maya. Raj brought the bicycle close to the bottom step and mounted it, planting his foot firmly on the step. Maya brought her soft behind in close contact with the hard metal crossbar and holding on to the handlebar lifted her feet from the stone step, to sit on the crossbar sideways. Raj had to balance their weights on the bicycle. He held the handlebar, and allowing Maya to lean against him he lifted his left foot from the step and pushed the machine forward, operating the pedals to gently propel the bicycle. After a few yards Maya shifted her weight slightly because the metal crossbar was quite hard. That slight movement disturbed their balance. Raj applied the brakes quickly but could not prevent the panic which now gripped them.

The bicycle gently tilted, depositing them both on the road. Neither was injured, only their clothes were covered in dust. They dusted themselves and, laughing quite heartily, walked back, first to Maya's house and then Raj on his own, went to his house. He freshened up, changed into clean clothes and talked quite freely about Maya to his mother. Raj's mother related the conversation to Raj's father, and both came to the conclusion that Raj was very much in love with Maya.

The very next day, after the failed crossbar attempt, Raj called at Maya's house, not only with his note files but also his bicycle. Maya opened the door and asked him into the house, where she introduced him to her parents and two younger sisters.

Maya's father was very impressed with Raj and from the behaviour of his elder daughter he got the impression that she was attracted to and even spellbound by Raj. Maya's father was a cultured, educated 'modern' judge, yet he was in some respects very reactionary. He silently decided to make enquiries about Raj's education, financial and caste status. He understood the new love-marriage movement in society and he was prepared to make concessions and allow his daughter to make a love-match, provided the young man belonged to the same Chitpavan Brahmin caste and had similar cultural traditions as his own family.

After making small talk with Maya's family and enjoying a cup of tea, Raj and Maya started to leave for the college. Maya had told her sisters in confidence about the crossbar ride attempt. 'Maya, don't try to get a lift on the bicycle,' shouted the younger sister. Raj and Maya glared at the girl, and Maya's parents were somewhat puzzled by the remark.

104

When the classes at college finished, Maya boldly asked Raj to let her try to sit on the crossbar. 'Let's try it in the college grounds,' he suggested. Maya firmly tied the end of her sari round her waist and sat on the crossbar, while Raj sat on the saddle and, resting left foot on the gravel forecourt of the college, set the bicycle in motion, keeping perfect balance. Fellow students watched this crossbar ride with interest and cheered encouragement. Raj operated the foot levers with confidence and did two rounds of the college forecourt. There was no accident this time and the pair got a lot of applause for this social and physical daring.

After a week's practice in the college grounds, Raj and Maya began to go 'double seat' in the level Pune streets. Their romance was the talk of the town.

Before the second year session came to an end, both families had got to know each other and held an official betrothal ceremony so that Raj and Maya could go openly together, either on foot or on Raj's bicycle. Both families made it quite clear to the couple that the wedding could take place only when both got their degrees. The final year's work would be the key to success.

Raj and Maya made arrangements to go riding at least three evenings each week and meet at Maya's house for study so Maya's mother would not have to worry whether Maya and Raj were doing secret sexual experiments. Although Raj and Maya displayed their love to the world, the world of the Brahmin community in Pune was small and narrow minded, and there was no possibility of any physical intimacy between even an engaged man and woman before the open and public wedding ceremony.

The last year in college seemed to fly past very quickly because Raj and Maya were very busy with their study and their 'togetherness'. In April 1951 the BA finals were over and the couple were at last free to enjoy the holidays in May. Both families had started hinting about the forthcoming wedding, the invitations, the preparations, the auspicious days for Hindu marriages. At first Raj and Maya both showed interest and even enthusiasm in the discussions.

One evening, as they were out enjoying their 'double seat' ride on Raj's bicycle, Raj suggested that they could climb the Parvati Hill and discuss what sort of a wedding they should really have. At the foot of the hill, Raj secured his bicycle with chain and padlock and they climbed the steps, holding hands and ignoring the censorious glances of the elderly men and women, and of not so old couples. They viewed the image in the Vishnu temple and walked to one corner of the temple courtyard to find a little privacy.

'Raj, our parents are planning a traditional Hindu marriage ceremony assuming that is what we want,' began Maya.

'Do you not want to experience the traditional ceremony then?'

'Not really. Look, India is now moving into a new age after Independence. Why can't we have a register marriage?' asked Maya.

'Because Society has certain rules and people expect to see a traditional Hindu marriage ceremony, especially in a traditional city like Pune,' said Raj.

'But we shall still be legally man and wife after the register marriage,' argued Maya. 'Besides we shall not spend all that money on the many traditional and sometimes unnecessary rituals.'

'We need to discuss this idea of a register marriage with our parents with the hope that they would accept the idea and give their blessings,' said Raj. They walked down the steps and, at Raj's suggestion, walked back to Maya's house. From there Raj cycled back to his house, hoping to persuade his parents to support their wish for a register marriage ceremony. The next day Raj spoke to his parents and suggested a meeting with Maya's family, and Maya spoke to her parents and suggested that Raj and his parents should be invited for a meeting to discuss the marriage plans. Maya took a note written by her father to Raj's parents and soon the meeting was arranged to take place at Maya's house in the morning of the Sunday of the following week. After the meeting, Raj and his parents were to stay to lunch.

When everyone had gathered in the main sitting room of the Judge's house, Maya looked around the room at all present, three visitors and four residents, and made an emphatic statement.

'I do not want a religious marriage ceremony. I want to have a register marriage. Raj feels the same way about it, I am sure.'

'Maya,' began her mother, 'we are Chitpavan Brahmins living in Pune. Society would expect a traditional Hindu wedding ceremony when both the bride and the bridegroom are of the same high caste. Register marriage is usually preferred when the parties are of different caste or even of different religions.'

Raj's mother seemed to support the views expressed by Maya's mother, but Raj's father supported Maya.

'I don't see any difficulty,' he said.

'Maya dear,' continued her mother, 'we have a responsibility to uphold and maintain our long-established traditions because we are Brahmins.'

'I don't agree,' responded Maya. 'We as Brahmins have enough influence in society to introduce new ideas, to set new trends. Towards the end of the nineteenth century, Professor Karve set a new trend and successfully paved

107

the way for "widow re-marriage" by himself marrying a widow. His personal action was not approved by Society for many years, but later Hindu widows from high caste families were able to remarry. Because we are supposed to be forward looking, Raj and I want to introduce and maybe popularise the idea of register marriage. Our marriage will be legal even without the chanting of the vedic mantras and the ghee offerings to Agni, the Sacred Fire.'

'Hear, hear!' said Maya's father. 'As a sub-judge, I can confirm that the register marriage is as binding as a religious wedding. I would support Maya and Raj in this new trend, but I shall miss the religious and the social elements.'

'We can have the social aspect of a Hindu wedding by having a feast dinner for all our friends after the register marriage ceremony,' said Raj's father.

'Nevertheless I shall be deprived of playing the important role as the mother of the bridegroom,' said Raj's mother.

After further discussion all agreed that Raj and Maya were to have a register marriage, that there would be a feast dinner for friends of both families and there would be the traditional exchange of saris and shirt pieces as gifts. The wedding was to take place after the Sankranti festival in 1952, probably around the last week in January. That would give both families ample time to book the marriage hall, make catering arrangements, send invitations and buy the gift saris.

Raj and his parents enjoyed the lunch after the 'planning meeting' at Maya's house, and the two younger sisters of Maya were delighted to hear that their older sister was going to make a love marriage and have a register ceremony.

Towards the end of the first week in June the BA degree results were declared, and Raj and Maya had scored high marks. They both wanted to be teachers so they registered for the teaching degree course at the New College in Pune and continued their 'togetherness' for the first two terms of the first year of their course.

Maya's parents were now very happy with the arrangements and decided to give an unusual gift to Raj, their first son-in-law. The judge ordered a motorcycle to be delivered after the Divalee festival so that Raj could learn to ride it during the holidays following the festival. When the brand new machine was delivered Raj and Maya were surprised and delighted. By the beginning of December 1951 Raj had learned to control the machine in the forecourt of New College and begun to go for a ride with Maya as a pillion companion. Maya found the new 'double seat' ride very exhilarating since she was able to encircle Raj with her arms and enjoy the body contact while sitting on a comfortable, padded seat behind him. It certainly was a change for the better from the hard crossbar ride on Raj's pedal cycle.

In north London, Jay and Lata were very fortunate to have established themselves within a year after arriving from Bombay. They had secure jobs and a secure place to live, and were determined to make a place for themselves in the country of their adoption.

They began to furnish and redecorate their flat. Both worked hard to paper the rooms and paint the woodwork inside the flat. Lata got advice from Mary Gupta about curtains and the many items needed in the kitchen to make their life comfortable. By the end of December 1951 the flat was fully furnished and they had the second bedroom and the box room ready for use. They toasted each other with coffee on New Year's Eve and enjoyed a very satisfying embrace, albeit with the presence of a baby-stopper. In the rosy glow of the post-embrace happiness, Lata brought up the subject of starting a family.

'Lata,' said Jay, 'you will have to continue to work up to seven months of pregnancy. That way you will be able to save enough money for the baby and for the housekeeping expenses for about six months. If all goes well, you will be able to rejoin the office when the baby is four months old.'

'I agree with your suggestion, but when shall we drop the baby-stopper?'

'Let's wait until after the Sankranti festival,' said Jay, caressing her cheek. In that happy state of mind they drifted off to sleep and when they awoke it was January 1952.

At the start of the New Year, Raj and Maya with the help of their families, made definite arrangements for the register office ceremony to take place on 28th January. Maya's younger sisters took charge of writing and posting the invitations to friends who lived in other cities and towns. The invitations to friends living in Pune were to be made in person by the couple's parents. The reception hall and the catering arrangements were finalised without much difficulty, which left ample time to buy the gift saris and other items of clothing.

On 28th January Raj, Maya and their families got ready in good time for the mid-morning ceremony at the register office. Raj and Maya offered homage to the god Ganesha and the family deities and sought blessings for a happy and long married life. At the register office they promised each other in the presence of the registrar and the witnesses to honour and cherish, to care for each other in health and in sickness, to remain with each other in affluence and in poverty, and to be sexually faithful throughout

110

their natural life. Then Raj and Maya signed the register. The two fathers also signed the register as witnesses. The marriage certificate was given to Maya because, in the absence of a public religious wedding ceremony, that was her only legal proof of her change of status.

At the reception hall, many friends gave their traditional 'saris and shirt pieces' gifts to the couple, and their parents gave gifts of equal value to all friends in return. Maya proudly showed her gold wedding ring and told her friends that she and Raj had exchanged rings like in a Christian wedding ceremony. But being Hindu Brahmins Raj had also given her a traditional marriage necklace of black beads worked in gold wire.

The feast lunch was well organised by the caterers and all the guests freely praised the variety and taste of the food. At the end of the day both families felt satisfied that the ceremony was a balanced mixture of innovation and tradition. Because the day had been very tiring and hectic, Raj and Maya decided to postpone their first ever sexual meeting until the last day in January.

The day after the register marriage ceremony, they had arranged to hold a typical Pune tea party for all their friends at the new college. At this tea party traditional savoury dishes like Bombay mixture, onion fritters and spiced boiled potato bhajee were served, which pleased all the guests. Maya and Raj were very popular with the students and the staff at the college because of their good looks and their innovative spirit which enabled them to introduce new ideas into their social behaviour without upsetting the traditional values like honesty, hard work and consideration for others.

On the last day of January the newly-weds arranged to be alone in Raj's house while his parents were out during the day. 'We should try our first intimate contact in the afternoon when we are both full of energy,' suggested Raj.

Maya enthusiastically agreed and said, 'I think a warm bath would help us to relax. What do you think, Raj?'

'I agree. Let's heat some water and bathe ... to —'

'Why do you stop?'

'If I say the word it might shock you, Maya.'

'Say the word ... and see if I am shocked.'

'Bathe together.'

'I'm not shocked. I'm very curious.'

'I suggested that because I think we should see each other without any clothes.'

'Why?'

'That will give you some idea of what you have to take into your body.'

They undressed completely. When the hot water was ready, they bravely and without any sense of shame bathed together, pouring water over each other and touching the other's body. At one point Raj was running his fingers over her secret opening, which made him grow bigger. Maya made a note of Raj's reaction. After drying themselves on soft towels, they went into Raj's room and stood on the mattress which was spread on the floor.

'I love you, Maya. I will not hurt you. You know that, don't you?'

'Yes, but it is going to hurt when you make me a woman.'

'Only because I'll have to use my weapon to break the thin curtain at the entrance of your secret passage. You must be brave.'

Raj then put his arms about Maya and holding her close to his body kissed her and gradually lowered her to the mattress. Natural instinct made Maya lie on her back and allow Raj to kneel between her opened thighs. He pressed his mouth on hers and, gradually moving closer to her, allowed his pointer to enter Maya's opening. Asking her to be brave, he pushed hard and breaking the barrier occupied her cave. The friction caused during the

112

'operation' made him lose control and within a minute his fluid was flowing into Maya while her core was feeling that tearing pain. As he withdrew and lay on his back, Maya's shame returned and she quickly left the bed and covered herself with the soft damp towel. A few drops of blood trickled from the battle scar on to the towel. She went into the bathing room and cleaned herself and dried her sore opening. Then she put on her underpants and, winding the towel round her middle, came back to the room and lay close to Raj, who caressed her and comforted her.

'I am now a woman,' she whispered, and they both lay quietly on the mattress and drifted off to sleep.

The start of February brought welcome news that their double room at a hotel in Lonavala, a cool hill station, was booked for one week. This was another gift from Maya's father, for their honeymoon. Raj and Maya rested that day, enjoying their new status as newly-weds and remembering the all too brief physical thrills that they had experienced during their first sexual encounter. Although Maya was a little tired and she felt a slight wincing ache every time she took a step forward, she glowed with an aura of pride that she had at last left her childhood behind and stepped into her new status as a woman.

Raj and Maya were to start their honeymoon on 3rd February 1952. Their luggage was packed and ready in a medium-sized steel trunk. On the day before, Raj, on the spur of the moment, decided to go for a motorcycle ride with Maya as far as the tunnel in the Katraj Hills on the Pune–Satara road. Raj's mother asked him to drive carefully as the motorcycle began to move forward. Maya put her arms around Raj to be in close body contact with him so that their combined weight would respond to the lateral movement of the machine and Raj would be able to maintain their balance at speed. They had no protective goggles or helmets since owning and riding a motorcycle was a new phenomenon in middle class families and the rules about helmets were not strictly observed or enforced. The rider and the pillion passenger felt energised by the wind on their faces. As the hills approached, the road became a little steep and Raj had to change to a lower gear to get more power. Soon they were riding along the winding mountain road and enjoying the swaying motion of the machine.

Raj slowed down because there were two bullock carts ahead of him. He waited and when he saw that the road ahead was clear he overtook both the carts just before a sharp bend. Another cart was coming on the other side, travelling towards Pune, and Raj did not quite manage to avert a glancing collision with it. He lost control of the machine and a few seconds later the motorcycle with both riders was tumbling down the steep side of the mountain, doing somersaults and depositing Raj and Maya in some thorny bushes. The machine continued its downward tumble and came to rest at the foot of the hill.

All three bullock carts stopped. The drivers and passengers got out and went up to the stone barrier wall and looked down. The two young city dwellers lay still. Two drivers got ropes from their carts, and while the passengers held one end of the ropes tightly, the two drivers slowly climbed down about fifty feet to the bush where the man and woman lay still and lifeless. Two more men climbed down to help. The four men with much effort brought the bodies up to the road and laid them on the ground. The young couple had died instantly as a result of broken necks. The driver of the bullock cart travelling to Pune agreed to take the bodies to the Sassoon Hospital and also to contact the police. Soon the two

114

carts resumed their journey towards Satara, 75 miles to the south, and the lifeless bodies of Raj and Maya were on their way to Pune.

Two hours later the bullock cart reached the hospital. The bodies were put on stretchers and taken to the emergency treatment room, where the doctors examined the bodies and declared them dead on arrival. Someone at the hospital remembered seeing the couple on a motorcycle near the New College, so the police sub-inspector sent one police constable to the college to find out who the dead couple were. The constable got the addresses from the college office and contacted the families. Raj's parents were stunned by the news. Maya's parents and sisters were speechless with grief. The sub-inspector wrote down the details of the accident as the bullock cart driver gave his eyewitness account. The police sent a truck to recover the damaged motorcycle and when the machine was examined, the official report of the accident was completed. It was late in the afternoon when the two families were able to get possession of the corpses and make cremation arrangements.

The news of the accident spread like wildfire and the staff and students were griefstricken to learn that the popular motorcycle-riding couple from the New College were dead. Maya's 'double seat' rides on Raj's pedal cycle were fondly remembered for the couple's daring social innovation and their fellow students remembered the happy couple at the college tea party. So much youthful energy and so much promise of the future were lost in a few seconds on the winding road in the Katraj Hills to the south of Pune.

Although Raj and Maya had had a register office marriage only the previous week, the funerary priest performed a full Hindu cremation ceremony on 2nd February near the river in Pune. Over two hundred people watched the pyres being lit and paid their final respects by taking leave of the young couple with tear-stained faces.

Destiny had motivated Ashok and Manjiri Joshi in Satara on 2nd February 1952 to make a baby. The same unknown mover had inspired Jay and Lata Bapat in north London, on the same day, to drop the baby-stopper and come together in a sexual embrace. As the funeral pyres blazed on the riverbank in Pune, the cracking of the skulls was heard by the people sitting close by.

The atman – the animating spirit – was released through the heat of the sanctified fire from Raj's remains. It winged in an instant to the room in Satara where Ashok and Manjiri had enjoyed a sexual embrace. The atman entered Manjiri's womb and became part of the baby-making fluid.

As the second skull cracked, the atman left Maya's burning remains and in an instant winged over five oceans and reached England halfway across the world and entered Lata's womb in Jay and Lata's flat in north London. Manjiri and Lata were not aware of the spiritual energy now fully established in their bodies. The two atmans that were unfulfilled in Raj and Maya were now re-housed in the new bodies being formed in Satara and London. Purusha, the life force, would be entwined with Prakriti – the matter composed of the five great elements: earth, water, light, wind and ether – to make a male child for Manjiri and a female child for Lata. For the present the two agitated and traumatised atmans were still and at peace.

While this spiritual renewal, devised and ordained by the Creator, was taking place in Satara and in London to rehouse the two atmans in new bodies, the families and friends of Raj and Maya in Pune were deeply immersed in sorrow and were unable to comprehend the Creator's design.

116

Step Five

On 3rd November 1953 Jay and Lata Bapat, living in their own unfurnished flat near Finchley Road station in north London, celebrated the first birthday of their daughter Meena. Meena was a well-formed, fair-complexioned baby who was born to Lata in New End hospital, Hampstead. Jay and Lata were now quite settled in their new country, had secure jobs and, had made many friends. They had kept in touch with Suresh Datye, who had travelled in the same ship with them. Mary and Ben Gupta were also present for Meena's first birthday party. As Lata picked her up in her arms from her carry cot, to everyone's astonishment, Meena spoke with a clear and confident voice.

'Mummy, I was the daughter of a judge in Pune, and was studying at the New College where I fell in love and married a young man whose first name began with the letter R. We both loved pedal cycles and motorcycles.'

After that, Jay, Lata and Mary tried to speak to Meena but she did not say a word. Everyone was surprised to hear Meena's story. Was she remembering some events from her previous life? No one could make out what possible connection there could be between one-year-old Meena and the two people she mentioned in her 'speech'.

Everyone enjoyed the savoury snacks and tea that afternoon. Three days later Jay wrote a letter to his brother in Pune giving the exact account of what Meena had said

117

and asked him to find out more details about her little story.

On 3rd November 1953 Baba Joshi and his wife Bai travelled from Wai to Satara by the early morning State Transport bus. At Satara they left the bus and walked to the rented house where their son Ashok and daughter-in-law Manjiri had lived since their marriage in April 1950. Not only were they well established in Satara but also Manjiri had given birth to a healthy and handsome son named Ramesh. Baba and Bai had made the special journey because Ashok and Manjiri had arranged a lunch party to celebrate Ramesh's first birthday. Ashok had also invited many of his Brahmin colleagues from the ST Depot.

Everyone had enjoyed the feast lunch and given their good wishes to the mother and baby. As Ashok distributed the betel leaf paan as a digestive aid and mouth freshener to his guests, Baba picked up one-year-old Ramesh. Suddenly there was a stunned silence as the little boy spoke to his granddad.

'*Ajoba* – grandfather – when I go to London I am going to marry a woman whose first name begins with the letter M. I shall never buy or ride a motorcycle. I first learnt to ride a motorcycle in the forecourt of the New College at Pune.'

Ashok, Manjiri and Bai tried to speak to the baby, but baby Ramesh never spoke another word that day. When he began to speak normally at the age of three, he never mentioned the motorcycle incident. Everyone was quite taken aback by Ramesh's 'speech'. Out of curiosity, Ashok wrote to a friend who worked for a newspaper in Pune, giving Ramesh's exact words, and asked the friend to find out the full story from the sketchy details.

118

*   *   *

In January 1954, Jay and Lata received a letter from Vijay Bapat, Jay's elder brother, who lived and worked in Pune. Jay and Lata read the full details of the story of Raj and Maya and were happy to learn the missing incidents from the brief summary given by one-year-old Meena. As Hindus, they had read about the transmigration of soul and the concept of successive lives passed by an atman in different bodies. They had only an outline knowledge of the philosophy behind the 'life after death' concept, so they did not probe the idea at length. They were satisfied to know that their daughter Meena had lived 'another life' in Pune. Meena had no further memory of her past existence, so Jay and Lata filed Vijay's letter carefully and after a few months almost forgot about the intriguing details of the story of Raj and Maya.

Also in January 1954, Ashok in Satara received a letter from his journalist friend in Pune. Manjiri was very much interested in the intriguing details of Raj and Maya's story since she had studied the philosophy behind the concept of successive rebirths which an atman has to experience to work out the effects and consequences of one's actions, commonly known as karma. Ashok and Manju learnt something about their son's past life in Pune and were puzzled as to why the memory of the past existence is very nearly wiped out as the person grows old and is completely rapt up in the present life. Ashok sent a hand-written copy of the letter to Baba Joshi, his father, and carefully kept the original letter in a steel trunk.

Time passed, weeks and months just flew past, and before long it was nearly the end of 1957 and Ashok and Manju celebrated Ramesh's fifth birthday. After the

119

birthday, Ashok and Manjiri visited Wai and discussed the idea of going to settle in London with Baba and Bai Joshi. They decided to make their plans after the Sankranti festival in January 1958.

Three days after the festive day of Sankranti on 14th January, Ashok wrote a letter to the officer in charge of the passport office in Bombay, requesting three application forms for passports. He felt satisfied that he had made a start to his emigration plan, and mentioned it to the Manager of the ST Depot where he worked. His boss was rather sorry that an efficient officer like Ashok would be leaving the service. At the same time he was pleased that Ashok was ready to improve his material prospects by going to settle overseas. Although Ashok Manjiri and their five-year-old son Ramesh would be facing an unknown world with a different climate, style of dress, unfamiliar food and a different language, he was secretly pleased that the family would escape the virulent anti-Brahmin atmosphere then prevalent in Satara. The Manager, being a Brahmin, supported Ashok's plan and offered to help in any way possible.

Ashok was surprised and pleased at the same time to receive the passport application forms quickly, along with a detailed list of the various papers that would be needed to accompany the applications.

Manjiri and Ashok studied the letter from the passport office and learnt that they would need domicile certificates, a report from the office of the District Superintendent of Police at Satara to say that the family were not involved in any crime, a certificate from the Revenue office at the District Collector's Department at Satara to say that Ashok did not owe any income tax and finally three passport-size photographs each of all three of them, duly certified by a notary public.

For the next two weeks Ashok was busy getting further

application forms for the necessary documents, visiting the DSP's office and the Revenue office and contacting the local photo studio. He was told that the application for a domicile certificate could be made at the Revenue office at Satara. Ashok's boss introduced the family to a senior lawyer who, being a notary public, would be able to certify the photographs. It was nearly the last week in February 1958 when Ashok got together the various documents and certified photographs. He was then able to send the application forms with all the necessary papers to the passport office in Bombay by registered post.

Ashok's boss suggested that initial letters of enquiry be sent to the Scindia Steam Navigation Company, the P&O line and the Italian Marine and Continental line to find out the possible sailing dates in July or August and the total fares from Bombay to London. Thus by the first week of March Ashok and Manjiri felt pleased that four important letters were on their way to Bombay.

After six weeks of hectic activity the couple spent four days to get a change of scene, visiting Nana Goray and his family at Sangli. Nana Goray, Manju's father, was very glad to hear the details of the emigration plan.

'Ashok,' he said, the day after their arrival at Sangli, 'I am very proud of your determination to leave India to improve your prospects, but you three are going to have some difficult months ahead, travelling, finding somewhere to live in London, getting jobs and possibly facing prejudice in England.'

'We realise that it is not going to be easy,' said Manjiri, 'but we are sure that the anti-Indian prejudice in England will not be as virulent and blatant as the anti-Brahmin atmosphere in western India in general and in Satara in particular.'

After a refreshing short visit to Sangli, Ashok, Manjiri and Ramesh returned to Satara. Ashok then wrote a detailed letter to his father about the applications for passports and about the letters to the shipping lines.

In the last week of March the shipping lines replied, giving the sailing dates of their ships and the fares for the entire journey. The ships of all three companies were to sail for England in July. The P&O fare was quite high, so Ashok decided not to consider that line. The Italian Marine and Continental line's ship was due to sail in the second week of July from Bombay to Genoa in northern Italy. From Genoa the company was going to arrange the entire journey, firstly by train to Calais via Paris, then by ferry to cross the English Channel to Dover, and the final leg would be by British Rail from Dover to Victoria station in London. The company's letter made it clear that the luggage would be handled by the company at Genoa, at Calais and twice at Dover, once from the ferry to the railway platform and, after the Customs check, on to the boat train at Dover, and finally at Victoria station from the train to the taxi. This service was included in the total fare from Bombay to London. Although the Scindia company's fare was about the same as the Italian company's charges, Ashok and Manjiri decided to try for a triple cabin in the Italian ship because the overland rail journey from Genoa offered a unique chance to see some part of mainland Europe and involved no extra or special effort. The fare per person was 67 pounds sterling, which would cost Ashok 871 rupees at the £1=13 Indian rupees rate of exchange. The Italian company was ready to accept the full payment of two and a half fares in rupees but the expenses on the ship would have to be met in lire. It was possible to convert rupees into lire on board the ship. There would be no need to obtain any francs while crossing France, since the train buffet would accept lire.

Ten days later the three passports arrived, which enabled Ashok to visit Bombay and book their tickets on the

Italian ship. Ashok decided to take Manjiri and Ramesh with him to Bombay so that the shipping company's booking officer would be able to identify the three passengers from their passports. Towards the end of April the family travelled from Satara to Pune by the State Transport bus and from Pune to Bombay by the early morning train. On both journeys they decided to take an overnight halt in Pune. Ashok carried with him sufficient rupees for the two and a half tickets on the ship, and for the return trip and food from Satara to Bombay. It was an exciting day for Ashok and Manjiri to book their passage to London and commit themselves to the 'once in a lifetime' adventure. When the passage was booked, the final departure from Bombay was just over two months away. They purchased two large steel trunks and one of a smaller size. The large trunks with their cotton and woollen clothes and some home-made spices could be stored in the hold while the smaller trunk could carry their 'wanted on voyage' clothes and shoes and sandals. Ashok was advised to carry no more than a couple of pairs of trousers and about four shirts. He would get better-tailored clothes in London. Manjiri was advised to take at least eight saris. As soon as the date of departure was known, their time was taken up in buying the various items for their adventure.

Manjiri's father had managed to make contact with two Brahmin friends and arranged a stay in Bombay for four days, both for the Goray family from Sangli and for the Joshi family from Wai.

All members of both families were on the dockside to wish 'bon voyage' to Ashok, Manjiri and Ramesh. The three passengers were garlanded and given a coconut each. They were asked to keep the garlands with them until they reached London but to offer the coconuts to the god Varuna with a prayer for the safe sea voyage to

Genoa. It was a moving goodbye for them all. Ashok, Manjiri and Ramesh were going to a strange land and Nana Goray and Baba Joshi suppressed their tears and sighs as they saw the three voyagers walk up the steps and board the TSS *Verona* of the Italian Marine and Continental line. 'TSS' was a short form of 'Twin Screw Ship'.

Ashok, Manjiri and Ramesh stood by the railings on the main deck and waved goodbye to the people on the dockside, as TSS *Verona* left Bombay harbour and the shoreline slipped further and further away. When the Indian shoreline had dipped below the distant horizon, they offered the coconuts to the god Varuna with a prayer for a safe voyage.

They located their triple cabin and were pleased to see their cabin trunk had been safely delivered. Ashok hoped that the other two trunks had been put in the ship's hold. They found out about the bathing and toilet facilities, the dining room and the middle deck specially set aside for the tourist class passengers. There was a shop where passengers could buy many articles to be used during the voyage. Ashok changed some rupees into lire notes and coins. He was careful to guard their sterling exchange, which would have to last them until he got a job in London. The biggest expense was going to be rent for a triple room in London.

All three suffered from seasickness until just before they were due to arrive at Aden after five days' sailing. When they were able to eat their meals without any sickness, they began to enjoy the voyage. There were two families with small children and Ramesh was able to make friends with three boys and two girls all about the same age as himself. The passage through the Red Sea was hot and uncomfortable. At Suez, the ship's navigation was taken over by a specialist pilot who took the *Verona* as far as Port Said. Ashok and Manjiri were very happy to experience cooler conditions when TSS *Verona* entered the Mediterranean Sea.

After sixteen days the ship reached Genoa, where all passengers had to disembark and continue their journey by train to various cities in Europe. Ashok noticed their big trunks as they were lifted up from the hold and put in the luggage compartment of the train bound for Calais. The train was specially reserved for the 'voyagers' so there was no need for it to stop at various stations on the way. It was a long journey from Genoa and they reached Calais after sixteen hours' travel.

Transferring to the cross-Channel ferry was another new experience, but the crossing was rough and they were glad to reach Dover. They disembarked and were directed towards the Customs area, where they had to identify their trunks and get them cleared. When their luggage was put on the train they took up their places in a second-class carriage.

It was the first week of August 1958 when they reached Victoria station. One family who had travelled on the ship had made arrangements to stay with Mrs Jacobs in Hendon. When they were met by Mrs Jacobs' son, Ashok asked him whether they could get a double or triple room at their house. Mr Jacobs said yes, and helped both the families with the luggage. It was sunny as Ashok, Manjiri and Ramesh, with their luggage, arrived at Mrs Jacobs' house in Hendon in north London. That was their 'journey's end'. As soon as their luggage was taken up to the large room on the first floor and a smaller single bed was arranged for Ramesh in the same room, their life in England began. They would get breakfast and evening meal at the house, but they would have to go out for lunch and tea or coffee, and Mrs Jacobs wanted £9 15s in advance for a week's stay.

When Ashok went out for lunch the next day he came across an Indian who spoke Hindi, was a student and lived in a house in Wembley owned by a Hindi-speaking couple. Ashok got the name, address and phone number of the couple in Wembley and made arrangements to visit the house the next day. Ashok and Manjiri did not eat meat or fish so they had to survive on bread, vegetables and milk at Mrs Jacobs' house.

Ashok, Manjiri and Ramesh arrived at the house in Wembley. When Ashok rang the bell, Mr Raam Tomar opened the door and said *namaste* in Hindi to greet the visitors and took them into his front room. Raam introduced his wife, Sita, to the visitors, and Ashok introduced himself, Manjiri and Ramesh to the Tomars and briefly explained that he was looking for some temporary accommodation where they could get vegetarian Indian food.

'You are in the right house,' said Raam. He had come to England nearly ten years previously from Patna, in Bihar, and had worked as a night shift worker in a laundry where the work was hard but the money was more than he would have got on some other labouring job. His wife worked in a plastics factory. When the Tomars had saved enough for a deposit, Raam was able to buy the three-bedroom house, and made the mortgage payments by keeping a couple of Indian students as paying guests, for whom Sita provided breakfast and evening meal. Every day, late in the afternoon, Raam did the shopping, and as soon as Sita came home, he went off to work in the laundry.

When Ashok told Raam that he had to pay £9 15s a week at Mrs Jacobs' house, Raam touched his own forehead and said, 'My God, people like that always exploit Indians – don't stay there more than a week. You three can use the large bedroom here and with meals it will cost you only £7 10s per week.'

Ashok was delighted to hear that the weekly cost was

going to be reduced by £2 5s. He reserved the room by paying one week's money, and when he went back to Hendon he told Mrs Jacobs that he, his wife and son would be leaving at the end of the week. Many months later, he was able to understand the true meaning of Raam Tomar's expression 'My God, people like that always exploit Indians.'

When the Joshi family were able to get vegetarian Indian food, life became a pleasure. Now Ashok was able to start his search for a job. He found Raam and Sita Tomar very honest, hard-working and kind-hearted.

Towards the end of August, Ashok found the location of the town hall from Raam and went to get some information about schools in the area. He was told that Ramesh could start his primary education during his sixth year. When Ashok told the officer Ramesh's date of birth, 3rd November 1952, the man gave Ashok some forms to fill in and asked him to come back in one week.

Ashok learned from Raam about the type of clothing needed in the winter when the weather would be cold and damp. The gas fire in the bedroom would be quite sufficient to keep warm but it would be expensive. Raam told Ashok that the family could sit in the dining room in the evening where there would be a coal fire, and Sita and Manjiri would be company for each other.

'You can experience some foggy evenings,' said Raam during their conversation, 'I think it is because most people burn coal for heating the house, and coal produces a lot of smoke which fills the air above London. I remember the great fog of London. It may have been either in 1952 or 1953. It was so thick you could not see anything beyond ten feet. It lingered for three or four days, and over four thousand old people died because of the sulphur in the fog. It was yellow-grey and it gave you a burning feeling in the throat.'

When Ashok mentioned that he was employed in the State Transport in India and was hoping to get a job with British Rail, Raam suggested that Ashok should go to Paddington station and get information about jobs on the railways. Following Raam's advice, Ashok went to the information office at the station and obtained three or four leaflets about jobs with the railways. That evening he examined the leaflets very carefully and discussed with Manjiri the type of job he should be looking for. There were vacancies for station porters, clerical jobs, apprentice drivers and train guards. Both he and Manjiri favoured some sort of office job. He wrote a letter of application for the job as a booking clerk at Paddington station and posted the letter the next day. To his great surprise he was asked to attend for an interview in one week's time.

The interviewing panel were interested in his experience in the transport industry in India.

'Well, Mr Joshi,' began the chairman of the panel, 'we can offer you a steady job as a booking clerk with wide travel concessions. It is a pensionable job.'

'Are there any promotion prospects?' asked Ashok.

'Yes there are. With your administrative experience, you could get a good promotion in the operations planning section. If you are interested in this job, you could start next week. The weekly wage would be nearly £12 with a free travel warrant card.'

Ashok accepted the job without any hesitation and filled in the official form immediately. Manjiri was very pleased to hear the news and hugged him when he came home in the afternoon. The Tomars were also happy to learn that he had got the job he was looking for.

That evening Manjiri discussed with Ashok the schooling prospects for Ramesh and her own wish to get a job to improve their material comforts. After discussing both these points with Raam and Sita the next day, Ashok and

Manjiri felt that they should stay in the Wembley area, and for the present continue to live with the Tomars until Manjiri got a job.

Ashok had filled in the necessary forms and he took them with him when he and Ramesh went to the education office. The officer in charge of admissions was a woman in her mid-thirties who advised that Ramesh could go to the local nursery school now, and after the Christmas holidays join the second year in the primary school as a special case – normally a child had to join a primary school after the fifth birthday.

When Ashok started his job in the second week of September 1958, a senior clerk showed him how to look up the stations, the fares and the trains from the various timetables and fare tables. He was given this intensive training for the first week. The following week he had to take part in a practical test, where three or four booking clerks posed travel problems involving obscure stations and train changes. Ashok answered all the questions and solved all the problem set for him. He was ready to man a booking office window from the next day.

He was happy to get his pay packet every Friday with a slip showing the National Insurance and income tax deductions. By the end of September he was able to meet all their weekly expenses without touching the reserve cash which he had brought from Bombay. He had to save money for the next couple of months to buy warm clothes for the winter and waterproof shoes for the three of them.

In the first week of October, Manjiri came across an advertisement for jobs in the large West London Hospital's office. With Ashok's encouragement, she wrote a letter of application and posted it the next day. For two weeks she waited for some response but was disappointed. Then in the last week of the month she got a letter asking her to attend an interview.

'Good morning, Mrs Joshi,' said the chairwoman of the panel of three, the other two being men. 'Take a seat and tell us briefly something about your background, education and family.'

Manjiri briefly outlined the necessary details of her life so far.

'Your English is good,' said one of the men.

'Thank you. It was one of the subjects for my language degree at Willingdon College, Sangli, in western India. The other languages were Marathi and Hindi.'

'Why do you think you will be useful in our hospital's records office?'

'I have a tidy mind,' replied Manjiri. The last remark reflected her self-assurance, which impressed the panel.

'You will start as a general clerk and after six months, if you prove your efficiency, you might get a promotion. The weekly wages will be £8 10s. You can start next Monday.'

Manjiri started her job the following Monday, which pleased her and made Ashok feel proud of her. Now their joint income would be just over £20 per week. By the end of November 1958 they had managed to buy warm winter clothes and shoes for the three of them. They decided to stay with the Tomars for the time being. Raam and Sita offered to redecorate the tiny box room and let it to Ashok so that Ramesh would have his own room and his parents could have privacy.

When Ramesh got his own room the Joshis could not believe their luck. 'You are a fortunate man, Ashok,' remarked Raam Tomar one day in November.

'Yes, I am. You know, Raam, Manju and I feel that it is better to be lucky than rich or clever.'

Raam laughed heartily to show his approval of Ashok's remark.

Just before the beginning of December 1958, Ashok

and Manjiri wrote letters to Baba Joshi at Wai and Nana Goray at Sangli, giving details of their good fortune in finding somewhere safe to live and also getting jobs to suit their temperaments. Nana Goray's letter arrived just before Christmas, offering congratulations on getting jobs and expressing his satisfaction at their good luck in their adopted land. Baba Joshi's letter arrived after the Christmas holidays. He was very glad that Ashok and Manjiri had got jobs and a safe place to live in London. He remembered Ashok's determination to settle in England, which he had expressed eight years previously, before he married Manjiri.

Baba Joshi gave news of their village which certainly justified Ashok's determination to escape from the virulent anti-Brahmin atmosphere.

My dear Ashok and Manjiri. We were very pleased to read your news, your success in finding jobs and your friendship with Mr & Mrs Raam Tomar. Your mother and I send our affectionate blessings to you all for success and happiness. Our love to Ramesh.

Three weeks ago Bai and I went to visit the temple at Dhoam, bathe in the Krishna river and imagine how the village looked before the house fires in February 1948. We went to look at the garden behind the temple but could see absolutely nothing. We were shocked. We stood at the barred gate and closed our eyes to see the scene as depicted on the screen of our memory.

We saw the neatly laid flower beds separated by paved paths, and with the iron water pipes with an opening at each bed and the wooden stoppers to control the flow throughout the large square garden. We saw the well in the corner which watered the flowering plants, shrubs, trees and the specially tended herbs and the medicinal herbs given free to those

131

who needed them to treat stomach aches, skin rashes, colds and fevers. We saw the tall bakul flower trees with their red berries, the delicate prajakta flowers, the holy rudraksha berry tree, the tall conifers, the yellow champak trees with their teak scaffolding which gave easy access to the golden blossoms, the green champak vine spreading over the roof of the shed above the well, the specially tended white ketaki plants with their captivating fragrances, multicoloured varieties of roses, red, pink, yellow and white, and many varieties of white jasmines. Every morning the Brahmin gardener with two young assistants picked flowers and put them in six shallow baskets in the temple for anyone to take a few and enjoy their beauty and fragrance. Many flowers were used in the village for the daily worship of the household deities in Brahmin houses. The cost of plants, seeds, fertilisers and labour was borne by a Brahmin family.

Because of this Brahmin influence and devotion to beauty, the village thugs took their revenge, emanating from the hatred of Brahmins in general and Chitpavan Brahmins in particular. They uprooted the flowering plants and shrubs, they cut down all those majestic conifers and golden champak trees. They dismantled the teak scaffolding round the trees and used it as wood fuel, along with the trees and plants. They dug up the paths, the metal pipes and turned the once pleasant and fragrant garden into a wasteland, a desert, a public urinal. There was no root, no twig, no leaf, no trace of what was. Deep-seated hatred turns humans into brutish savages and makes them blind to beauty.

I am writing this with painful memories at the loss of that once pleasant plot, knowing how much you loved that garden. Never mind! Never look back. One day you can make your own garden. Indeed you made a wise decision to settle in England. You have now got steady jobs and Ramesh will be educated in state schools. So, some time next year obtain British nationality by registration. Then you will put down roots in your adopted country and flourish through honest hard work.

With blessings,

Your affectionate father
Baba Joshi

P.S. After looking at the devastation of that plot, we came back to the Narasimha-Vishnu temple and sat in front of the shrine. From there we saw the solid circular stone pillar in the middle of the lotus-shaped pond, above it the large stone tortoise, on its back, the attractive temple of Nandi, the bull, in front of the Shiva temple. Looking at the stone tortoise brought fond memories of the week-long intense activity of you and your childhood friends in filling the pond with water at the time of the annual festival. Those pleasant memories soothed our troubled hearts.

Ashok read and re-read his father's letter with choking grief at the loss of the garden.

Step Six

The month of December 1962 was cold and on some days it was damp, not because of rain but because of mist and fog. Jay and Lata Bapat and their daughter Meena had lived in their flat near Finchley Road station since September 1951. Meena was born in November 1952 and in that cold December of 1962, she was in the final year at her local primary school.

Ashok and Manjiri Joshi and their son Ramesh were settled in the house owned by Raam and Sita Tomar in Wembley by the end of December 1958, just four months after their arrival from Bombay. Early in 1959, following his father's advice, Ashok had applied to the Home Office for British nationality by registration for the three of them. By June of that year the Joshi family had got their British nationality and passports. Ramesh had joined the local primary school in Wembley at the start of 1959. The following year when Ashok and Manjiri had been confirmed in their respective jobs and Ramesh had got used to the school, Ashok and Manjiri felt that they should get a rent-controlled unfurnished flat in the Wembley area. They discussed the matter with Raam and Sita, who supported their idea and offered to help.

It was June 1961 when Ashok managed to find the flat he was looking for. He had already saved money for buying the necessary furniture. When he got the keys from the estate agents, he and Raam Tomar closely examined the two-bedroom flat with a large reception room, kitchen/dining room, toilet/bathroom and generous storing cupboards. Raam and Ashok thoroughly cleaned the flat and hung new wallpaper in three rooms and painted the kitchen, bathroom and the little entrance hall using emulsion paint. Ashok got a big carpet for the living room and small carpets for the bedrooms. After the beds and mattresses and the sofa and two armchairs were delivered, Ashok and Manjiri moved in in August 1961. Raam Tomar helped to move their belongings to the new flat, which was not very far from the Tomars' house. The Joshis were indeed lucky to have settled in London within three years after their arrival from Bombay.

Ashok had installed gas fires in the main reception/living room and the two bedrooms, and 'cheap rate' night storage electric heaters in the kitchen, bathroom and the entrance hall. His foresight with the gas fires and heaters paid handsome dividends when the whole of Britain was in the grip of the 'Big Freeze' between Boxing Day 1962 and 14th March 1963.

The snow fell on Boxing Day and many people in London, where the snow had not lasted in the past for more than a week, said with confidence, 'We will be all right before the New Year. This won't last for more than a week.' This human optimism was thoroughly undone by Nature with her icy-cold tentacles as they spread over the land and water. Nothing escaped the freezing invasion. Roofs, gardens, roads, cars, buses, railway tracks and rolling stock were covered with snow, ice and frost. Walking became very dangerous. Hospitals treated hundreds of patients for ankle or wrist fractures as men, women and children slid and slipped on ice.

There were delays and hold-ups for public and private

transport. Car drivers carried newspapers or old sheets and snow shovels to rescue their vehicles from snow and ice. This common calamity melted the normal British reserve and people actually talked to other people without being introduced, and there was no colour or race bar during these spontaneous conversations. If a motor vehicle was stuck or was sliding on ice, people volunteered their help to push the car till it moved under its own power. People who had to park their cars in the road outside their houses had reserved their place by clearing the snow and ice from a patch to park the car. Many hot words were exchanged if someone parked their vehicle in another's 'reserved' ice-free space.

Trying to keep warm and keeping one's car and the pavement outside free from snow and ice became a major occupation. Water pipes froze, car batteries became flat, and freezing fingers, dripping noses and freezing breaths were common occurrences. One elderly lady from London had to travel by train to visit her grandson who lived in Leicester. She wanted to know whether there would be buffet service on the train. When the station porter replied, 'Yes madam, but no 'eating,' she was more than puzzled.

There was also white, stupefying fog on some days. Driving became pretty difficult and confusing. One driver in the fog noticed bright tail-lights of a car in front and decided to follow it, hoping to hit a clear patch. When the leading car stopped, the follower also stopped. The driver of the first car got out and spoke to the other driver.

'I don't know where you want to go, mate, but I'm in my garage.'

Such were the trials and tribulations of the 'Big Freeze'.

Fortunately, the Joshi and Bapat families had no accidents on ice and managed to keep warm and follow their occupations, and the youngsters did not miss school except for four or five days when the weather was too cold and the schools were officially closed. The local councils managed to clear the snow from the main roads in London but the side roads remained frozen for the duration. When 14th March 1963 brought mild conditions and the snow and ice melted, everyone breathed a sigh of relief and the British regained their normal reserve and went back to the usual practice of saying 'good morning' to particular acquaintances and ignoring the rest.

In July 1963 Meena had completed her primary school education and, having passed her eleven-plus examination, she was given a place in the local grammar school. Ramesh had also secured a place at the local grammar school in the Wembley area. The parents of both the children were taxpaying citizens since all four had regular permanent employment.

There was a regional cultural association of Marathi-speaking people who had come to Britain from the State of Maharashtra in western India. The association did not have any permanent place of its own, for lack of funds, but hired a church hall in north London to hold a variety of programmes to preserve the Marathi culture in an alien environment. On these occasions, which numbered about eight in a year, many Marathi-speaking families made friends with other families. The British-born generation of Hindus was given a glimpse of their parents' cultural heritage through these regular 'get-together' afternoons/evenings. In the beginning most of the cultural events, including music, drama or celebrations of Hindu festive occasions, tended to cater for the parents' nostalgic hankerings and the children were inadvertently left out because most of the programmes were conducted in the Marathi language.

In January 1966, the Marathi friends circle in London had organised a get-together afternoon at their usual church hall in north London to celebrate the festive occasion of Makara Sankranti, when the sun crosses the Tropic of Capricorn in its apparent northerly journey. This is a harvest festival in some regions of the Subcontinent. On this day, in western India, people visit friends and neighbours and exchange a preparation made from sesame and gurr – raw sugar – to renew close ties. There was no organised entertainment programme at this gathering. It was meant for people to meet their friends who perhaps lived in other cities, renew earlier friendships, and make new friends.

Ashok and Manjiri met Jay and Lata for the first time.

'Hello, I am Ashok, this is my wife Manjiri. We live in Wembley.'

'Hello, I am Jay, this is my wife Lata, and we live in the Finchley Road area.'

Jay and Lata had been in London for nearly sixteen years, while Ashok's family had come to London in 1958. Lata and Manjiri got on well with each other, and Lata invited the Joshi family for lunch on the last Sunday in January.

At the same gathering Ashok met two persons he had met on the day of his marriage to Manjiri at Sangli in 1950.

'Hello Ashok, do you remember me?' asked a stranger who seemed to know Ashok.

'I'm sorry, I don't recall our meeting.'

'I'm not surprised after such a long time. I am Manohar. We met on the day you got married at Sangli in 1950.'

'Oh, yes, I remember now. There were four of you there and you had made a special visit to meet me. I think you were in medical college,' said Ashok.

'Yes, I qualified in 1955 and came to London in 1959.

138

Since then I have moved to Reading, where I practise as a GP.' Manohar then introduced his wife Prabha to Ashok and Manjiri, and to Jay and Lata.

Manohar asked Ashok, 'Do you know what happened to the other three persons I met at Sangli?'

'Yes. There was Arvind, who came from a Chitpavan family in Ichalkaranji. He qualified as a civil engineer and now he lives and works in North Carolina State in the USA.'

'There was a young man called Madhav, whose father was a temple priest at a town called Narsobachi Wadi near Kolhapur,' remembered Ashok.

'That's right, he became an accountant and now lives and works in New York.'

At this point, another Chitpavan Brahmin came over to Ashok and Manohar.

'Hello Ashok, I'm Rajendra. Hello, Manjiri. My sister was in your class at Sangli. I became a doctor and now practise as a GP in Birmingham.' Then he introduced his wife Nalini to the others.

At the close of the Sankranti day in north London, Ashok and Manjiri and Jay and Lata had met Manohar and Prabha, who lived in Reading, and Rajendra and Nalini, who lived in Birmingham.

On the last Sunday in January 1966, Ashok, Manjiri and Ramesh travelled by bus and underground to reach Jay and Lata's flat at about eleven in the morning. Meena opened the door and when she saw Ramesh she simply stood in the doorway speechless, bewildered and slightly confused by some memory which flooded her mind for a few seconds.

Lata came into the hall and spoke. 'Meena, darling, aren't you going to invite our guests to come into the house?'

'Yes, mum, I was just going to,' said Meena, moving away as the three visitors came into the hall.

Lata closed the front door, and Jay came into the hall from the kitchen and smiled at the guests as a gesture of welcome. He took their coats and asked Meena to take them to the main bedroom.

'Would you like tea or coffee?' asked Lata. All three visitors asked for tea. As Lata went into the kitchen to make tea Meena followed her.

'What happened, Meena?'

'Nothing, I thought I was somewhere else.'

'You are here in London, and when I make tea, you can help me carry the cups into the sitting room.'

While the mother and daughter were busy getting tea, Ashok and Manjiri were led by Jay into the tastefully furnished sitting room.

'Welcome to our flat,' said Jay.

'Thank you. Our flat is very similar,' Ashok said.

'Ramesh, which school do you attend?'

'The grammar school in Wembley – I am in the fourth form,' responded Ramesh.

'It is not so cold today,' observed Jay. 'It was bitter around Christmas. I thought we were going to have another freeze-up like 1963.'

'No thanks,' said Manjiri. 'That freeze-up will last us for a few years.'

At this point Lata and Meena came into the sitting room carrying tea and biscuits. Meena gave the cups of tea and biscuits to Ashok and Ramesh, while Lata gave tea to Manjiri and Jay. As Meena handed Ramesh a cup, he closed his eyes and imagined himself to be somewhere else. That unseen hand from the past touched Ramesh for a few seconds and then he was back in the present, accepting tea from Meena and saying 'Thank you'.

'Meena,' asked Manjiri, 'which school do you attend?'

'The local grammar school. I am in the fourth form,' replied Meena.

'You and our Ramesh seem to be of the same age. When were you born, Meena?'

'In November 1952 in London.'

'So was Ramesh, on 3rd November 1952 in Satara,' explained Manjiri.

'Where is Satara? Is it in India?' Meena asked.

'Yes, it is south of Pune in the Marathi-speaking state called Maharashtra.'

As everyone had their tea, Lata and Manjiri collected the cups and saucers and went into the kitchen. Manjiri offered to help but Lata had all the work under control. The food was nearly ready, only the rice had to be cooked. While Lata got busy with the rice, Manjiri stayed in the kitchen and talked to her. Ashok and Jay exchanged details of their family backgrounds in India and their present jobs in London.

Meena had asked Ramesh to go to her room, where he could look at her books and the ornaments on the mantelpiece. This was the first time Meena had met Ramesh yet she felt that she had known him all her life. He was well built at fourteen, with a light complexion and distinctive green eyes. He is like me, she thought, because she also had a light complexion and green eyes. Ramesh was reading the titles of her books and examining the glass and china ornaments on the mantelpiece while she drank in with her eyes every tiny detail of his physique and face.

'Meena,' called Lata.

Both the youngsters went into the kitchen. Lata, Meena, Manjiri and Jay carried plates and cutlery and various dishes of food into the sitting room, where there was a table set for six persons.

Lata had prepared spiced vegetable curry, spiced lentils,

chappatis, rice and finely chopped cucumber with grated roasted peanuts and natural yoghurt as a typical regional relish. She had roasted six papadams and had the mild mango pickle jar ready if anyone wanted it. Manjiri read the label on the pickle jar and said that she also got all the spices and pickles from the same shop near Euston station. Everyone enjoyed the lunch and in a relaxed atmosphere got to know each other. Lata made tea for the guests before they left just after four, when it was quite dark.

'I like Ramesh,' Meena told her mother when they were doing the washing up.

The journey back home for Ashok, Manjiri and Ramesh was slow since they had to wait longer for buses on that Sunday afternoon.

'Meena is beautiful,' said Rarnesh as they reached their flat in Wembley.

Ashok and Jay, both having been brought up in the Chitpavan Brahmin families, had almost identical social and cultural patterns of behaviour. The idea of honest hard work to earn a living was second nature to them. Living within one's means has been a typical Chitpavan trait for centuries and this quality of frugality and prudence has often been wrongly interpreted by other Brahmin sub-castes and non-Brahmin castes as 'Chitpavan stinginess'. But in matters of family or national importance the Chitpavans will be generous to a fault and they are known to have suffered privations and terms of imprisonment in fighting for a just cause.

In August 1968, Manohar and Prabha Saane decided to celebrate the tenth anniversary of their marriage. They had twin daughters, Jaaee and Juee, who attended the local primary school, and Manohar was a respected doctor

142

practising as a GP in Reading. They planned to hold a small gathering of Chitpavan Brahmin families by inviting Ashok, Manjiri and Ramesh Joshi from Wembley in north London, Jay and Lata Bapat with their daughter Meena from Finchley Road in north London and Rajendra and Nalini Khare with their son Prasad, who lived in Birmingham.

The two families from London didn't have far to travel. Since Ashok was now a senior booking officer working for British Rail at Paddington station, he was able to get a group return ticket for the four adults and two children at a reduced cost. Ashok and Jay with their families arrived before eleven at Manohar's house in Reading, about half an hour before Rajendra, Nalini and Prasad, who drove to Reading from Birmingham. This was a joyous occasion for Manohar and Prabha, and the others had come with suitable gifts for them.

The new generation had been born in Britain, except Ramesh, and they quickly made friends with each other. Manohar and Prabha had decided to order chicken and chips from the nearby takeaway chip shop and bought lots of fruit drinks and ice cream from the supermarket. It saved the labour of cooking, and the menu was going to be a hit with the younger generation. Manohar had stocked up with beer, lager and white and red wines.

As soon as the visitors from London arrived, Jaaee and Juee, the five-year-old twin daughters of Manohar and Prabha, went to the front door and joining their palms and slightly bowing welcomed them with the word 'Namaskar'. This traditional welcome by the girls impressed and amused the visitors. Manjiri and Lata affectionately pecked the girls on the cheek in appreciation and everyone entered the house.

Ashok and Jay opted for lager, while Manjiri and Lata preferred tea and Ramesh and Meena chose orange squash. The hosts made small talk by asking about the comfort of the train journey and commenting on the sunny weather of the day. Soon the three guests from Birmingham arrived and Rajendra and Nalini said hello to everyone, while Prasad, their four-year-old son, asked for 'owenge dwink'. Juee gave him his 'owenge dwink' with much amusement. Soon the twins and Prasad were asking Meena and Ramesh to go into the garden. Lata quietly asked Meena to take care of the youngsters as they had to navigate some stone steps leading from the French window down to the lawn. Prabha made a cup of tea for Nalini, while Rajendra was happy to accept a glass of lager from Manohar, who also poured a glass for himself.

'Here's to a happy get-together,' said Manohar, and the rest responded with enthusiasm. 'Listen everyone,' began Manohar, after sipping his lager deeply, 'the children are in the garden and our lunch of chicken and chips will be delivered just after half twelve, so we have time for some serious stock-taking of our present and future lives in Britain in view of some frightening political statements by a senior Tory politician.'

'Our future is in Britain,' said Rajendra. 'We need not be frightened because the ideas put forward by the speaker are not likely to be put into practice. We have taken out British nationality by choice. Four out of our five children were born here and are British by birth. Where will they be sent if repatriation schemes get the backing of the British Government and the British people?'

'We are needed as part of the workforce here,' said Ashok. 'Manohar and Rajendra are doctors. Jay is an employee of a firm of architects, I am on the permanent senior staff of British Rail. Manjiri works in hospital administration and Lata works in a successful estate agent's office. Besides, the views expressed by the speaker do not represent the views of the Government or Parliament or the vast majority of the British people.'

144

'Let me add two more points,' said Manohar. 'We emigrated from western India to Britain to get away from the poison of the anti-Brahmin, anti-Chitpavan atmosphere. There are dozens of Chitpavan families settled in the UK. The dominant anti-Brahmin caste in Maharashtra burnt our houses and now we have burnt our boats, so to speak. So we all have to fight and stem this vicious racist wave by the democratic method.'

'How do we do that?' asked Lata.

'By not voting for the known or suspected racist candidates in the local or Parliamentary elections, and by avoiding people or situations where you will get a lot of racial abuse; a favourite phrase these days is "a f*****g Paki". People of South Asian origin are an easy target because they are all of small stature and, more importantly, they are competitors. I have experienced this myself.'

'Britain is known for tolerance and fair play,' said Rajendra, 'so we need not fear as long as we continue our Brahmin tradition of being law-abiding useful citizens.'

There was a ring at the door. The lunch had arrived and almost at the same time all children came into the house, as if they had smelled the chicken and chips. Suddenly the seriousness of the previous half an hour had given way to a happy family gathering. Rajendra, Ashok and Jay gave their gifts to Manohar and Prabha before the buffet lunch. Meena noticed that while she was being protective and caring towards the twins and Prasad, Ramesh was rather aloof. Yet after spending a day in the company of very young children, Meena found that Ramesh was warm hearted and really wanted to be with her. On the return journey they got their chance of sitting next to each other and indirectly learning each other's likes and dislikes.

* * *

145

Between January 1966 and August 1968, Meena met Ramesh three times. Some unknown magnet had drawn her to him.

In the last week of August 1968 there were inter-school swimming galas in north London which were to take place over three days. Ramesh and Meena had completed their GCE 'O' levels in June of that year and were waiting for the results. So both were free to take part in the swimming competitions. They arrived at the open-air swimming pool with their school parties and quickly changed into their swimming clothes. Ramesh and Meena, being sixteen, were in the last but one competition. This was strictly segregated, so that Ramesh competed against boys of his age and Meena competed against girls of her age. They both admired each other's bodies while waiting for their races.

Ramesh seemed to have become stronger in the previous two years and Meena was mesmerised by his muscular body. Ramesh looked fixedly at Meena and saw a very beautiful well-developed young woman.

Ramesh watched as Meena swam like a mermaid and won her event with ease. Then he had to face stiff competition but he managed to come second in his event. As they separately went into their cubicles to change and dry themselves, the thin film of water dropping from their bodies seemed to clear the present from their memories. Each one had many questions which needed answers yet the pressure of the present kept these answers hidden in the deep recesses of their past life.

As Ramesh removed his trunks and dried himself, his mind probed into his memory bank. Where had he seen that lovely face, those soft plump lips, those well-formed breasts and thighs? He felt the enchanting pressure of those lips on his lips, of those well-developed breasts against his chest and the close contact of those thighs

146

against his thighs. But where? Not in this life. This was the very first time he had seen Meena in her attractive light blue swimming costume, yet he had that nagging feeling of past experience which the secret compartments of his memory bank refused to unlock.

As Meena removed her swimming costume and dried herself, many questions crowded in her mind. Where had she felt that manly mouth upon hers? Where had she pressed her yearning breasts against his chest? Where had she felt his hands gently caressing her back and breasts and buttocks? Where had she experienced the ecstasy of his kiss? Those questions pulled her mind towards her memory bank but the bank door would not open and the questions remained unanswered.

Ramesh and Meena did not have any time for a friendly chat that afternoon since they had to board their separate school coaches and return to their homes.

One week later Meena got her GCE 'O' level results. She had passed in seven subjects, getting grade A in English language, maths, physics and biology and grade B in chemistry, history and geography. Her parents were delighted with her progress.

'What did your career teacher suggest?' asked Jay.

'I am good in maths and science so I have been advised to choose three or four subjects for "A" level, which would lead me towards a degree in science or medicine,' replied Meena.

'I am afraid I won't be able to support you for the expensive medical course,' said Jay, 'but a degree in science or pharmacy will be within our reach.'

'I would like to be a pharmacist so that I can be independent by having a chemist's shop of my own in the future,' replied Meena.

'A good idea, darling,' said Lata.

After getting further advice from the teachers, Meena

started her GCE 'A' level studies in maths, physics, chemistry and biology.

Ramesh had passed his 'O' levels in six subjects. In the half-term break Jay, Lata and Meena were invited to spend a day with Ashok, Manjiri and Ramesh. Meena longed to see Ramesh again.

When they arrived at Ashok's flat, Meena got that certain feeling as soon as she saw Ramesh. Her feelings swelled up in her chest when Ramesh very cunningly shook her hand when she least expected it. During the very mundane activities, like laying the table for lunch, collecting food dishes from the kitchen after lunch and helping with the drying of the plates and cutlery after Manjiri had done the washing up, both Ramesh and Meena became aware of each other's physical presence and both longed to hold hands.

'Ramesh, could we walk up to your school?' asked Meena.

'Yes, certainly. Let's get our coats.'

Soon they were walking away from the flat, instinctively holding hands and exerting gentle pressure on the other's hand to send a secret signal. As Meena looked at the school building through the railings she noticed that Ramesh's school in Wembley was very similar to her school in Finchley. Ramesh's hand comforted her hand, and when they were standing by the railings their shoulders touched. As they turned their heads towards each other, their aromatic and spicy breaths intermingled for a few seconds before their lips came together. This was their first fleeting kiss, which did not express any passion, but there was a promise of tomorrow in it. When they got back to the flat, Manjiri and Lata looked at them closely but found no signs of budding emotions.

After that enchanting day Ramesh and Meena immersed themselves in their studies and their lives progressed separately. Ramesh had passed six GCE 'O' levels, namely

148

English language, maths, history, geography, chemistry and biology. Following his career teacher's advice, Ramesh chose maths, chemistry and biology for his 'A' level course.

Meena passed four 'A' levels with good grades and secured admission for a degree course in pharmacy, starting in September 1970. Ramesh got admission to study for a BSc degree in maths, chemistry and biology after his 'A' level results 1970. Although they progressed separately, their lives were going to be intertwined.

The London Marathi club held a Diwali dinner function in November 1970, when Meena had been in her college for nearly two months. Ramesh and Meena both became eighteen years old in that November and when they met at the Diwali function, Meena expressed her love for Ramesh.

'I love you, Ramesh.'

'I love you, Meena.'

Then they kissed passionately in front of everyone. Those mutual declarations broke the ice and during the evening their parents were made aware of the delicate bond that had grown between Ramesh and Meena over the previous two years.

'Listen, darling,' said Lata to Meena, 'your father and I are very happy for you but you must complete your studies first.'

'Yes, Mum. Ramesh and I have agreed on that point. We'll get our degrees first and then consider the next logical step.'

When Ramesh told his parents that he loved Meena and wanted to marry her, Ashok and Manjiri were delighted to hear the news but asked Ramesh to complete his studies first. 'Of course, Dad. Meena and I have agreed on that point.'

Since Ramesh Joshi and Meena Bapat came from

Chitpavan Brahmin families, they were equal on social, cultural, educational and economic levels. Their parents could not possibly object to their eventual marriage. Although they were British nationals, culturally they were Hindus and both families would want a full Hindu wedding for them.

In the third week of August 1973, Meena received her degree result. She had passed with an upper two grade. She was over the moon.

'Well done, darling,' said Lata as she hugged her daughter and kissed her on the cheek.

'Well done, Meena. Congratulations,' said Jay as he shook her hand.

Meena phoned Ramesh that evening to give him the good news.

'Congratulations, Meena,' said Ramesh.

There was another surprise for her that evening. Jay told her that she could visit Bombay and Pune for about six weeks and meet her grandparents on both sides as well as Uncle Vijay and his family.

'You would enjoy sightseeing in Bombay and the railway journey to Pune. It will be an ideal opportunity for you to visit the family in Pune at the time of Diwali festival in November, and you will miss the monsoon rains,' said Lata.

The very next day Jay contacted an Indian travel agent and booked a return air ticket to Bombay. Meena's flight was scheduled for 14th October, which gave her about five weeks to prepare for her trip, buy suitable cotton clothes for herself and small presents for the various relations in Pune. Her passport was valid for another three years.

Days passed quickly and busily for Meena and her

parents, and on 14th October she boarded the plane at London airport for the 'unknown' world of Bombay and Pune. She promised to send a telegram from Pune as she said goodbye to Jay and Lata.

The economy section was half full and the journey took ten hours, including a short stop in Abu Dhabi. Jay had written to his brother Vijay about Meena's visit and Vijay had been waiting at Santa-Cruz airport for Meena, whom he had never met; but he had brought her photo with him to make identification easy. The flight from London landed about two in the afternoon and as soon as Meena had come through Customs, Vijay and his wife met her. They travelled by taxi to Victoria Terminus and boarded the fast train for Pune. They arrived at Pune station at eight and reached her grandparents' house in half an hour. After a welcoming ceremony she was introduced to her grandparents and Vijay's son Nandu and daughter Maala. It had been an exciting, tiring day and soon after the evening meal Meena was fast asleep.

The next morning Vijay sent a telegram to Jay and Lata informing them of Meena's safe arrival. Meena found herself in a world which was familiar and at the same time very strange, as she wrote to her parents after she had been in Pune for nearly two and a half weeks.

Pune
5th November 1973

Dearest Mum and Dad,

I had a very comfortable flight between London and Abu Dhabi. When the plane stopped there for about one hour, many passengers got on and it was clear that the airline had overbooked. In the centrally located seats in the economy class the aircrew had to put two extra persons per row where there were

151

supposed to be only six persons. The passengers were not complaining and were happy to put up with discomfort for a few hours as long as they got to Bombay.

When I got out at Bombay, I felt a heat wave wafting over me. It was also very humid and the overhead fans were not cooling the air, just whirling the warm air around the arrivals terminal. I got in the queue and had my completed immigration form and my British passport ready. The policeman at the counter looked at me, looked at my passport and said, 'You are called Meena Bapat. How can you be British?' I simply pointed out that I was born in London. I don't think he was convinced. I told the Customs officer that I was visiting my grandparents in Pune for Diwali and that it was my very first visit to Bombay. 'Have you any electrical items such as a radio?' No only clothes, I told him. When he put a chalk mark on my suitcase, I went out of the terminal into the open forecourt. It was very bright and very hot.

Uncle Vijay and Auntie Leela spotted me and approaching me, Uncle Vijay said, 'You are Meena. You look exactly like your photograph.' He insisted on taking my suitcase as we got a taxi to go to the railway station called 'Victoria Terminus' but I noticed that everyone referred to it as VT. Uncle Vijay had got our tickets in advance so we made our way to the correct platform and got on the train which is called the *Deccan Queen*. It was cool inside the train. I was hoping to see a bit of the countryside from the train but it became quite dark after we had sped past Kalyan Junction. The journey through the mountains was quite cool. When we arrived at Pune station, I noticed that the air was not so humid as it was in Bombay. When we arrived at the Bapat family house, grandmother Tai – whom I have learned to call 'Tai-aji' – put a dab of red kum-kum on my forehead and rice grains on my head and waved a ghee lamp in front of me to ward off evil from my life. Then I met grandfather – Dada-ajoba – and my cousins Nandu and Maala. We had our evening meal rather late. I was very tired and was glad to lie down on a mattress-bed on the floor.

In the few days I have been at Pune, I have met Mum's parents, whom I now call Appa-ajoba and Mai-aji. I am very happy to be in Pune, surrounded by so much affection from my four grandparents.

Another thing I had to learn was the use of water instead of paper after visiting the lavatory. Now I know why Indians avoid the use of the left hand in the preparation of food and when giving and receiving anything. The left hand is 'spiritually' unclean although physically not dirty when I use soap and water to wash my hands after the toilet visit.

I find Pune very noisy and there is litter in some streets, just as some streets in London are full of litter and discarded plastic containers. I can't get used to the crowds and I have noticed that in side roads there is an oppressive smell of human and animal urine and excrement. There are no adequate toilet facilities in public areas. Many persons in my age group tend to speak English mixed with many Marathi words, and Nandu and Maala have told me that I speak Marathi with a London accent. I shall have to learn to read and write Marathi when I return to London.

On my birthday, 3rd November, Auntie Leela bought me a sari, petticoat and blouse and taught me how to wear them. It was a novel experience. I went with Nandu and Maala to the temple on the hill, which is dedicated to the goddess Parvati. I also visited the Shiva and Vishnu temples there.

When we were about to start to climb the broad steps I was overcome with a most peculiar sensation that I had been there before. For a few seconds I felt the presence of a young man who was similar to Ramesh. I simply sat down on the second step and held Maala's hand for support. That certain presence of the past soon vanished. I recovered from the sensation and we three climbed the steps, visited the temples and made our *namaskars* to the deities in homage.

In those few forgetful seconds I spoke words which have little meaning for me. Nandu said that I was saying 'The crossbar is hard.' Maybe it was the influence of the day!

I am enjoying myself and looking forward to the festival of Diwali.

With love

Yours, *Meena*

Two days after receiving Meena's letter from Pune, Jay and Lata got a letter from Vijay.

Pune
8th November

Dear Jay and Lata,

Meena has written to you giving her impressions of Bombay and Pune. We are all very happy to have her here for Diwali, which we will celebrate in another ten days' time. On 3rd November it was Meena's birthday and Leela taught her how to wear a sari and blouse. Meena looked very beautiful in her sari. When they went to visit the temple on the hill, Meena

154

appeared to be in 'another world' for a few seconds. Nandu and Maala were with her and they told me that Meena, in her 'forgetful seconds' was saying the words 'The crossbar is hard.' Jay, do you remember I sent you a newspaper cutting after Meena's first birthday? Maybe her 'forgetful seconds' are somehow linked to her past life. I am sure there is nothing medically wrong with her, but to allay our anxiety, I am going to take her to our family doctor for a, general check-up. Meena has told us about Ramesh Joshi, who has got his BSc degree in London. Is he her link with her past life? Dada and Tai are keeping well. Next week Leela, Meena, Maala, Nandu and I are going to spend a day in Bombay. We shall make the return trip by the *Deccan Queen* train.

With best wishes,

Yours, *Vijay*

Vijay had booked five return tickets on the *Deccan Queen* train and had the seats confirmed before they started their journey from Pune. Meena was pleased to be travelling during the daylight hours and was amused to see the metal girders carrying the overhead power cables all rushing back to Pune. 'Uncle Vijay,' she asked, 'did the Mughals or the Marathas build the Indian railways?'

'Neither. Thank God it was the British who built the railway network. Otherwise we would still be in the bullock cart age.'

'But Dad, said Maala, 'we are still using the bullock carts in the villages.'

'We have to,' said Nandu, 'because even thirty thousand miles of railway track does not reach all the towns and cities. Now the State Transport buses connect many towns, but to get to the villages, we have the reliable bullock cart.'

Meena was learning something new about India. The train soon reached Lonavala, where a second engine was coupled at the back, which provided the extra power needed to pull the train up the steep gradient and also gave better control when travelling downhill. Meena was impressed by the rugged scenery and the engineering skill that was necessary to lay the track by drilling many tunnels through the basaltic rock of the Western Ghats.

Pune was cool and the air remained cool throughout the mountain journey. When the train began its descent towards low-lying Bombay, the air warmed up quite a lot and it was humid as well. Fortunately the whole train was air-conditioned so the humidity did not affect the traveller until the train reached Dadar station. Many passengers left the train there but some went on to Victoria Terminus. At VT, Vijay and others left the train and slowly made their way along the platform through the jostling crowd. It was just as well that they had no luggage otherwise their progress out of the station would have been even slower. Meena was quite overwhelmed by the human mass. She held Nandu's hand and followed. 'So many people!' she said as they came out of the station.

'We'll have some tea first,' said Vijay as he led the way to a café.

'What do we do now, Dad?' asked Maala after tea.

'We'll go to Kaalaa Ghodaa and visit the museum.'

'Uncle, what is Kaalaa Ghodaa?' asked Meena.

'There used to be a statue of King Edward VII on a black horse. The statue disappeared in new India but the bus stop is still known as Kaala Ghodaa,' explained Vijay.

'Why did they get rid of the statue? Was it because it was ugly?'

'No, it was quite imposing – it was a reminder of British rule.'

'When will the Government in India get rid of the

156

railway system and the post and telegraph department? Are they not permanent reminders of British rule?' asked Meena.

'That's different,' replied Vijay evasively.

Meena enjoyed her visit to the museum. After about one hour they walked towards the Gateway of India. 'Who built this solid stone structure?'

'The British, of course.'

'Are we getting rid of it?'

'No, it was paid for with Indian money and Indian labourers' sweat. That's why it will stay,' replied Vijay.

Leela was quite impressed by Meena's bold and logical questions. She suggested that they should all go to a vegetarian restaurant for lunch.

'Are we going to the Taj Mahal hotel?' asked Meena.

'No, we can afford to look at it from the outside only.'

Although it was early November, the Bombay weather was hot and humid. Fortunately there was air-conditioning in the modestly priced restaurant and they spent nearly two hours savouring their lunch in cool surroundings. After lunch they took a six-seater taxi and went to the Malabar Hill to walk in the Kamala Nehru Park, where they admired the topiary figures shaped from privet hedges.

'Auntie Leela,' enquired Meena, 'who was Kamala Nehru?'

'She was the wife of Jawaharlal Nehru, the first Prime Minister of Independent India.'

'Isn't Indira Gandhi the Indian Prime Minister? Is she the daughter of Mahatma Gandhi?'

'No, no, no. Indira Gandhi is the daughter of Pandit Jawaharlal Nehru. Mrs Indira Gandhi was married to Feroze Gandhi, who was an architect by profession.'

After a pleasant walk in the park and an interesting lesson in recent Indian history for Meena, it was time to walk down a few steps to the waiting taxi to go back to

VT and board the *Deccan Queen* for the return journey to Pune.

'It was a very interesting visit to Bombay but a very tiring day, Uncle Vijay,' said Meena after they got back home in the evening.

Meena particularly enjoyed the Diwali celebrations because Dada-ajoba and Tai-aji explained the religious significance of each of the five days of the festival. Her grandparents explained everything in Marathi, but when Meena found Marathi words difficult, either Nandu or Maala translated them into English.

In early December Meena said goodbye to her relations in Pune with tear-filled eyes as she boarded the plane to fly back to London. She cherished the deep affection which had surrounded her during her first visit to Bombay and Pune, and was happy and proud to show the photographs, two weeks after her return, to her parents, friends and to Ramesh.

She spent a day with Ramesh during the Christmas vacation. When she told him of her 'forgetful seconds' in Pune she felt that he understood the impact of the words 'the crossbar is hard'. They kissed deeply and passionately and spoke of their love for each other, and returned to her home. In the New Year she got a job as a trainee pharmacist with a well-known pharmaceutical company.

In June 1973 Ramesh sat the degree finals in London and when the results were declared in August he was glad to read the letter from the university that he had passed his examinations with an upper two grade. Ashok and Manjiri were delighted. Ramesh and Meena celebrated the event by going out to have a meal and by confirming their love for each other.

'I want you,' Ramesh said.

'I'll be yours on our wedding night.' Meena firmly made the promise.

In November 1974, when both were twenty-two, Ramesh and Meena got engaged with their parents' full approval. Both families agreed that the wedding would be celebrated in London.

'I want a religious ceremony,' said Meena.

'So do I,' said Ramesh, 'with English translation of all the mantras.'

Ashok and Jay had made enquiries when they realised that their offspring would marry. Ashok contacted Pandit Gopal and invited him for a meeting with all interested parties to discuss the wedding plans, and Jay contacted the managers of a couple of halls to ascertain whether they would be available in June or July of 1975. He had made a tentative booking for July of both the halls, hoping to seek others' approval and then confirm the booking of one hall. So the stage was set for Meena and Ramesh to form a partnership. Meena was progressing as a trainee pharmacist but Ramesh was still looking for a suitable job.

Step Seven

In the first week of December 1974, soon after Meena and Ramesh were officially engaged on their twenty-second birthdays, Pandit Gopal, the priest, came to the flat where Meena and her parents, Jay and Lata, lived. Ramesh and his parents, Ashok and Manjiri, had arrived half an hour earlier.

The priest was welcomed by Meena and Ramesh, who offered the traditional greeting by bowing before him with their palms joined in front of them and speaking the words *namaskar guruji*, a term of respect.

'May you be blessed with a long and healthy life,' said the priest, blessing the couple.

'After tea and refreshments, Pandit Gopal was told that the couple did not know Sanskrit and furthermore, they were unable to read and write their parents' mother tongue, Marathi. But both families wanted an abridged Vedic wedding. Then the priest gave a brief account of his family background and priestly training in western India and explained how he would conduct the ceremony in July the following year.

'I was born into a Brahmin family in southern Maharashtra. My father was a priest who could not afford to send me to college after I had passed the SSC examination and left school. I was trained to be a priest in the Vedic tradition by my father and two other scholarly priests. Then I came to London and got a job as an assistant to

160

a friend of mine who runs a successful newsagent's shop in north London. My job in the shop gives me a steady income and I supplement that by conducting various religious ceremonies for Hindu families. I charge a moderate fee for the auspicious rituals but conduct funeral services free. I also visit other cities and towns for my priestly duties. I shall recite the Vedic mantras, giving their source, and use mantras from the Puranas for the pre-wedding *puja*, then read the English translation prepared by my learned friend, Mr Hemant Kanitkar. I shall announce the translator's name before the ceremony so that his copyright will be protected.'

Pandit Gopal then advised about the materials and utensils needed for the wedding ceremony.

After the day of the marriage was agreed upon, Jay confirmed one hall booking for July by paying the deposit, and arranged for the Mandap – the ceremonial framework with awning and decorated chairs for the wedding day.

Jay and Ashok sent sponsorship letters to their respective parents to enable them to travel to London and attend the wedding ceremony in July. Although traditionally the bride's family bears all the expenses of the ceremony, Jay and Ashok had agreed to share equally all the costs of the wedding. There was much activity in the two households during May and June when the families had to gather all the materials for the wedding and also buy special presents by way of saris and shirts for the various relations and friends. One week before the ceremony, Jay's parents, Dada and Tai Bapat, arrived in London. Two days after that, Ashok's parents, Baba and Bai Joshi, also came to London.

The day before the wedding ceremony, Meena and Ramesh had the register office ceremony in the morning and Pandit Gopal performed the *puja* of the family deities and the god Ganesha at Jay's flat, attended by both families, in the evening.

Pandit Gopal, wearing the ceremonial clothes of a Hindu priest, arranged the altar in the main reception room so that the worshippers would face east and the *murtis* – of the Mother Goddess and the god Ganesha – would face west. On the altar, which was covered by red cloth, he put a few grains of rice under the images and under the water vessels. Two ball-shaped copper vessels were half filled with cold water, and a few grains of rice, a betel nut and a copper coin were put in them. A coconut was placed on each vessel and five betel leaves were placed under the coconut so that the pointed ends of the leaves protruded outwards. The copper vessels were decorated with dabs of red kum-kum and yellow turmeric and represented the seven holy rivers of Hinduism, namely Ganga, Yamuna, Godavari, Sarasvati, Narmada, Sindhu and Kaveri.

Sipping water

The priest then asked Jay, Lata and Meena and also Ashok, Manjiri and Ramesh, to sit beside the altar, in that order. Each person was asked to sip water as *guruji* spoke three names of the god Vishnu. On the fourth name the water was put on the right palm and allowed to trickle into the copper tray placed on the floor. As everyone joined their palms in front of them in a gesture of reverence, *guruji* recited twenty more names of Vishnu. The sipping of the water was for spiritual cleansing.

Regulating breathing

The next ritual involved regulating the breath to increase concentration. The nostrils were closed by the thumb or the little finger of the right hand. Breathing started through the left nostril by closing the right one, then both were closed for holding the breath, and the air was breathed out only through the right nostril, keeping the left one closed. The process was repeated by breathing in through the right nostril, holding the breath and breathing out through the left nostril. Breathing was thus regulated while *guruji* recited, first the mystic words, then the Gayatri verse from book three of the Rig Veda. 'We concentrate our minds upon the most radiant light of the Sun God. May the Sun God stimulate our intellect.'

Homage to various deities (aspects of the supreme spirit Brahman)

The worshippers joined their palms in front of them while *guruji* chanted Sanskrit verses offering homage to gods and goddesses. 'I offer homage to the god Ganesha, to the family and personal deities, to the deities of the town and the house. Homage to all the gods and goddesses, to all the learned persons present, to the main deities worshipped in this ceremony; to the heavenly bodies, the sun, the moon and the planets Mars, Mercury, Jupiter, Venus, Saturn, Rahu and Ketu.'

Verses of praise

Pandit Gopal read the translation after the Sanskrit recitation.

'Whosoever recites or hears the twelve names of the god Ganesha, will have no obstacles at the start of the study of scriptures, at the time of marriage, or other ceremonies, when entering or leaving any building, during an armed conflict and when undertaking a difficult task. In order to dispel all obstacles, meditate upon and offer worship to the god Ganesha, who has four arms, a pleasing face, a moon-like complexion and is wearing white garments.'

'I offer *namaskar* in homage to the Great Goddess, who

163

enhances the auspiciousness of everything lucky, is good luck incarnate, is the protector of a devotee, who is also called Tryambaka, Gauri and Narayani.'

'Those whose hearts are dedicated to the god Hari (Vishnu), the abode of All Bliss, find that all their endeavours are blessed with good luck.'

'I offer silent homage to the divine feet of the husband of Lakshmi (Vishnu) because that moment of remembrance is the essence of auspicious time and day, of the power of the planets and the moon, of wisdom and of providence.'

'Those whose hearts are dedicated to the god Vishnu (Janardana), having the dark complexion of a blue lotus, become prosperous and achieve success. They know not any failure.'

'To attain fulfilment in all actions I first offer *namaskar* and homage to Vinayaka (Ganesha), Jupiter, the Sun God, Brahma, Vishnu, Shiva and the goddess Saraswati.'

'I offer *namaskar* and homage to the god Ganapati, who removes all obstacles and who is worshipped by other gods and even demons to attain fulfilment of their wishes.'

'May the Lords of the three worlds, Brahma, Vishnu and Mahesh (Shiva), crown all our undertakings with success.'

Announcing the exact time and place of the ceremony

The priest put in appropriate words from the Hindu almanac to fill in the blanks.

'In the measured time brought into existence by the command of the Great God Vishnu, today in the second half of the long period of the god Brahma's life span, in the god Vishnu's abode, during Brahma's day known as *shwetavaraha*, in the period named after Vaivasvata Manu, in the first quarter of "Kaliyuga", in the 28th era, in England, in London to the north of the river Thames, in the saka era named after King Shalivahana, in the present year named ——, during the northerly/southerly movement of the sun, in the —— season, in the Hindu month of —, in the light/dark half, on the —— lunar date, on —— day, when —— constellation appears in the sky, the sun, the moon and other planets being in various zodiacal houses.

Intention and purpose of the ceremony

Jay declared the purpose of the ceremony: 'On this auspicious lunar date I perform the sacrament of marriage of my and Lata's daughter Meena to Ramesh, son of Manjiri and Ashok, to enable the bride and the bridegroom to fulfil the aims of *dharma* (social and religious duty), *artha* (earning a living by honest means) and *kama* (enjoying the good things of life), all in moderation.

'I shall offer *puja* worship to the god Ganesha and to the family deities to seek their blessings.'

Jay and Ashok both spoke the invocation mantra after the priest.

'I invoke the god Ganesha to be present here with his consorts, retinue, power and weapons to receive the worship and bless the couple.

'I invoke the Mother Goddess to be present here with her consort, retinue, power and weapons to receive the worship and bless the couple.'

Then all six persons in turn offered red kum-kum, yellow turmeric, rice grains, flowers, sacred thread, food, fruit, betel leaves, incense and light to the *murtis* and offered homage and prayers. Then the two water vessels were duly consecrated with the appropriate mantras, chanted by the priest.

'In these vessels may the gods Vishnu, Shiva, Brahma and the mother goddesses be present. May the spirits of

165

the oceans, the earth, the Vedas and allied scriptures be present here. May the other gods and goddesses be present here to remove all evil. May the spirits of the river goddesses Ganga, Yamuna, Godavari, Sarasvati, Narmada, Sindhu and Kaveri be present in these vessels.' The water vessels were then offered red and yellow powder, rice grains and flowers in worship.

Jay and Lata picked up one vessel and brought it in contact with Meena's forehead to bring her the blessings of the river goddesses. Ashok and Manjiri touched Ramesh's forehead with the other vessel for the same purpose.

Pandit Gopal, the parents and grandparents of the couple expressed a wish that the ceremony be successful without any difficulties and the wedding day be auspicious. Then *guruji* told the people that the mantras for the pre-wedding *puja* were taken from a Purana text, dating from the 10th century AD. These were also translated by Mr Kanitkar.

The wedding day

'My name is Pandit Gopal and I, as the officiating priest, welcome you all ladies and gentlemen, to this Hindu marriage ceremony. Meena and Ramesh have chosen each other, so some would call this a love marriage. The *mandap* and the area around it is to be treated as holy and leather footwear must be removed.

'Today's ceremony includes essential religious rituals and the mantras – sacred prayers – are mainly from the Rig-Veda and the Aashwalaayana and other Grihya Surtras, the earliest Hindu holy books. The ancient Sanskrit mantras are sacred and deserve your respect. You are honoured guests invited to witness this serious and holy marriage ceremony. I request you to observe complete silence while the mantras are recited. Then, and only then, will everyone hear the words and understand the significance of the rituals. Meena and Ramesh will try and speak the Sanskrit mantras in some rituals. I shall read the English translation of the mantras prepared by my learned friend Mr Hemant Kanitkar. Then the service will become meaningful to young Hindus born here.

'The altar in the *mandap* has consecrated statues of the Mother Goddess and the god Ganesha. There are two water vessels representing the holy rivers of Hinduism. A full pre-wedding *puja* was performed yesterday. I shall now invoke the god Ganapati and Meena's parents will sip water and offer a short *puja* to the deities.'

1) *Invocation of Ganapati* (Rig-Veda 2.23.1)

'We call upon you (Ganapati), the leader of the assembly of gods, the divine priest, the scholar among scholars, first among the knowers of Brahman, of incomparable fame. Hear our prayer and grace this place (of ceremony) with your all-protecting presence.

'Now that Jay and Lata have spiritually purified themselves by sipping water three times, and offered the short *puja* to the deities, ladies and gentlemen, I have to request you to voice your support for and approval of this ceremony. Please repeat after me, as loudly as you can, three phrases in Sanskrit.

'Om punnyaaham – May the day be auspicious
'Om Swasti – May everything be well
'Karma ridhyataam – May the ceremony be successful.'

2) *Private worship of Parvati and Shiva*

'Thank you ladies and gentlemen for your support. The bride, Meena, is offering private worship and prayers to

167

Parvati and Shiva to seek blessings for prosperity, long married life, good health and sons and daughters.'

3) *Seemaanta Pujan*

After the invocation, Ramesh and his parents and grandparents were welcomed at the door of the hall by Meena's mother and grandmother with a sacred light to ward off evil spirits. This ritual is called *seemaanta pujan* – the welcome at the boundary. As Ramesh was brought into the hall and given a seat ot honour, a Sanskrit verse was recited in praise of the god Vishnu, because on this day the couple are likened to Vishnu and his consort Lakshmi:

'I offer *namaskar* to the god Vishnu who removes fear from daily life and who is the Lord of the universe. He is the husband of Lakshmi, has lotus-like eyes and is mediated upon by the *yogins*. He has a divine body the colour of a cloud. He is limitless as the sky and protects the world. He is the chief among the gods, has a serene appearance and lies on a many-headed serpent.'

4) *Madhuparka*

Then Jay gave Ramesh a little honey to sweeten the welcome.

Jay: I give this honey in welcome to this bridegroom who having completed his scriptural studies has come to my house to seek my daughter's hand in marriage.

Ramesh: With the inspiration from god Savita, with the arms of the Ashwins, with the hands of god Pushana, I accept this honey.

Guruji: Ladies and gentlemen, while Ramesh is enjoying

the honey, as the officiating priest, I shall recite a mantra from the Veda (Yajurveda: 13.27 Vajasaneyi Samhita):

'May the breezes be sweet (pleasant); may the rivers flow with sweet waters; may the herbs give us sweet (soothing) fluids; may the night and dawn be sweet (comfort us); may the extent of the earth be sweet; may our father sky be sweet; may the plants (and fruit) provide sweet juices; may the sun be sweet (not fierce – to make us healthy); and may our cattle give us naturally sweet milk.'

5) *Kanya-dana*

After this, Meena was formally given in marriage by her parents and accepted by Ramesh and his parents. In this ritual three generations of ancestors of the young couple were mentioned three times by name.

Jay repeated Sanskrit formula after the priest. To this young man born in the Joshi family, the great-grandson of ——, the grandson of ——, the son of Ashok and Manjiri Joshi, Ramesh by name, I give in marriage this bride, born in the Bapat family, great-granddaughter of ——, granddaughter of ——, daughter of Jay and Lata Bapat, Meena by name, in order for her to attain the status of a married woman and to fulfil the aims of *dharma, artha* and *kama.*'

Ramesh touched with his right hand the right shoulder of Meena and said, 'I accept this bride in marriage.' Then the couple stood facing each other. Meena sought a promise of moderation from Ramesh. He promised accordingly. The mantras from the Grihya Sutra were repeated three times by the couple.

Meena: Dear friend, you must not offend against me in your observance of *dharma, artha, kama* (i.e. you must be moderate).

169

Ramesh: Fortunate one, I promise to be moderate in *dharma*, *artha* and *kama*.

The parents of the couple stood before each other and promised friendship between the families.

6) *Expressing three wishes*

Meena and Ramesh then took some rice grains in their left hands and, standing facing each other, expressed their dearest wishes which they hoped would be fulfilled during their married life.

Meena: May I be blessed with *good fortune*.
Ramesh: (showing support by putting a few rice grains on her head) So be it.

Ramesh: May I be able to perform fire sacrifice and other *religious rituals*.
Meena: (showing support by putting a few rice grains on his head) So be it.

Meena: May I be blessed with *wealth*.
Ramesh: So be it.

Ramesh: I hope to perform my *dharma* well.
Meena: (with some grains of rice) So be it.

Meena: May I be blessed with *children*.
Ramesh: (with some rice grains) So be it.

Ramesh: I hope to be *successful* in my work.
Meena: (with some rice grains) So be it.

Guruji: (putting a few rice grains on the couple's heads) May all your dreams and desires be fulfilled in your married life.

7) *Amulet on the wrist*

Soft cotton thread with turmeric root was tied by Ramesh round Meena's left wrist and by Meena round Ramesh's right wrist as the priest recited the mantra:

'This amulet is the marriage bond and it will exorcise evil spirits, will enable the couple's relatives to prosper and will bind the couple in mutually dutiful affection.'

8) *Marriage necklace*

Ramesh then fastened a necklace of black beads round Meena's neck to bring them good fortune, affection and life-long friendship.

'I place this beautiful and auspicious necklace symbolising good fortune, love and affection, and friendship, round your neck, my bride.'

9) *Holding the bride's right hand*

Then Ramesh took Meena's right hand in his right hand and said the mantra (Rig-Veda 10.85.36), 'I hold your hand, my bride, to bring us good fortune. I hope you grow old with me as your husband. The gods Bhaga, Aryaman, Surya and Indra have entrusted you to me so that I may fulfil my duties as a married householder.'

10) *Marriage Homa (fire worship)*

The young couple gave oblations [*aahutee*] of holy darbha grass to Skanda; of five pieces of sacred wood from banyan, pippal, udumber (Indian fig trees), mango and palasha (*Butea frondosa*) to Agni (God of Fire); and then three offerings of ghee to Prajapati, Agni and Soma, and with longer mantras, four oblations of ghee to Agni. These offerings complete the main *Homa*.

Prayers were also offered for prosperity, food, welfare of domestic animals, children, for keeping enemies at a safe distance, for long life, grandchildren and for mutual love and affection between husband and wife.

A controlled fire was lit in a metal container using pieces of wood and camphor. The couple sat facing the fire, the bride on the right-hand side so that she could touch the bridegroom's right hand with her right hand as he made the offerings to Agni. The bridegroom with three blades of darbha grass purified the materials by sprinkling them with water.

Ramesh: I establish the sacred fire, yojaka by name, in the metal container. (As the flames rise, a prayer is offered to Agni.)

Ramesh: O Vaishwanara Agni, of Shandilya gotra, having a banner with a ram emblem, being in the east in front of me, grant me a boon. May this oblation of dharbha grass reach god Skanda.

The couple offered the sacred wood to Agni. 'O Jataveda Agni, this wood fuel is your atman. May you burn vigorously because of it. May your power increase. Likewise, may our children, our cattle, and our knowledge of Brahman increase. May we be blessed with plenty of food (and water) through your grace.

Now that this fuel is given to Jataveda Agni, it is no longer mine. (Aashwalayana Grihya Sutra 1.10.12.)

Seven ghee oblations (put in fire):

Ramesh:

i) I give this ghee oblation to Prajapati, the Lord of creatures.

ii) I give this ghee oblation to Agni, God of Fire.

172

iii) I give this ghee oblation to the extinct plant, Soma.

iv) Ramesh (Mantra – Rig-Veda 9.66.19): Oh Agni, you purify our lives. Provide us with food. Keep harm far away. Now that the oblation is given to Agni, the Purifier, it is no longer mine.

v) Ramesh (Mantra – Mantra Brahmana 2.1): May Agni, the foremost among the gods, be present here. May he release the bride's future children from the snares of death. May god Varuna be pleased with her and prevent her from mourning her sons and grandsons. I give this oblation to Gaarhapatya Agni. It is no longer mine.

vi) Ramesh (Mantra – Hiranyakeshi Grihya Sutra 19.62): May the Gaarhapatya (household) Agni protect this bride. May he grant long life to her children. May she be the mother of living sons. May she experience the happiness of seeing her grandchildren. I offer this oblation to household Agni. It is no longer mine.

vii) Ramesh (Mantra – Rig-Veda 5.3.2): You are Aryaman, the nature of women, and you have a secret name, O self-directed One! They anoint you with milk like a well-made contract, since you make husband and wife to be of one mind. I give this oblation to Agni. It is no longer mine.

11) *Offering of roasted rice/millet*

The couple gave three oblations of roasted rice/millet to Aryaman Agni, and to the gods Varuna and the sun, with prayers for increasing their love and affection, and dutiful friendship for each other. After each offering they circumambulated the sacred fire. Meena was then asked to stand on a stone slab and be firm as a rock to defend her honour and her new family's honour. The ends of the couple's upper garments were tied for this ritual.

First oblation (Mantra – Aashwalayana Griha Sutra 1.7.13)

Ramesh: The bride has offered worship to Aryaman Agni. May Agni weaken her ties of affection for her natal family and strengthen her ties for her husband's family. The oblation is given to Aryaman Agni. It is no longer mine.

Circumambulation of fire and water vessels (Mantra – Aashwalayana Grihya Sutra 1.7.6)

Ramesh: My bride, I am Sky, you are Earth. I am the melody of the Sama-Veda, you are the verse of the Rig-Veda. Let us marry and have children. Dear to each other, radiant, well-disposed. Let us live for a hundred autumns.

Stepping on a stone slab (Mantra – Aashwalayana Grihya Sutra 1.7.7)

Ramesh: My bride, step on this stone slab. Be firm as a rock. Boldly face your enemies and defeat them (to protect your own and your new family's honour).

At this point the bride's brother twists the bridegroom's right ear to remind him of his duty of care towards the bride. He is given a token gift.

Second Oblation (Mantra – Aashwalayana Grihya Sutra 1.7.13)

Ramesh: The bride has offered worship to the god Varuna. May Varuna weaken her ties of affection for her natal family and strengthen her ties for her husband's family. Now that the oblation is given to the gods Varuna and Agni, it is no longer mine.

174

Circumambulation (Mantra – Aashwalayana Grihya Sutra 1.7.6)

Ramesh: My bride, I am Sky, you are Earth. I am the melody of the Sama-Veda, you are the verse of the Rig-Veda. Let us marry and have children. Dear to each other, radiant, well-disposed. Let us live for a hundred autumns.

Stepping on a stone slab (Mantra – Aashwalayana Grihya Sutra 1.7.7)

Ramesh: My bride, step on this stone slab. Be firm as a rock. Boldly face your enemies and defeat them (to protect your own and your new family's honour).

Third oblation (Mantra – Aashwalayana Grihya Sutra 1.7.13)

Ramesh: The bride has offered worship to the Sun God and to Agni. May the Sun God weaken her ties of affection for her natal family and strengthen her ties for her husband's family. Now that the oblation is given to the Sun God and to Agni, it is no longer mine.

Circumambulation (Mantra – Ashwalayana Grihya Sutra 1.7.6)

Ramesh: My bride, I am Sky, you are Earth. I am the melody of the Sama-Veda, you are the verse of the Rig-Veda. Let us marry and have children. Dear to each other, radiant, well-disposed. Let us live for a hundred autumns.

Stepping on a stone slab (Mantra – Aashwalayana Grihya Sutra 1.7.7)

Ramesh: My bride, step on this stone slab. Be firm as a rock. Boldly face your enemies and defeat them (to protect your own and your new family's honour).

Ramesh: I offer the remaining millet to the Lord of Creatures. This is now offered to Prajapati. It is no longer mine.

12) *Sapta-padi – seven steps*

Ramesh and Meena sat on chairs and waited while the priest put on the floor small heaps of rice grains in a line to the north of the sacred fire. The couple stood side by side, Ramesh's right hand on Meena's right shoulder. Both did a short slow march, always starting with the right foot, and walked seven steps together. Before each step, Ramesh spoke the mantra:

Ramesh: O my bride, support me in all my undertakings. May god be your guide.

Meena: I will support you in your righteous undetakings.

This mantra was repeated before each step. Both took one step forward with the right foot and brought the left foot forward to stand still before speaking the mantra for the next step. The heaps of rice grains were markers.

Ramesh: Take the *first step* for a plentiful supply of *food*.

Take the *second step* to give me *strength*.

Take the *third step* to increase our *wealth*.

Take the *fourth step* to increase our *happiness*.

Take the *fifth step* for children. Support me in my endeavours. May we be blessed with many *sons and daughters*. May they live to a ripe old age.

Take the *sixth step* so that we may enjoy seasonal pleasures together.

Take the *seventh step* for a life-long friendship and companionship.

The newly-weds were then sprinkled with water by the priest. Ending the ceremony by the bride's parents. One more oblation of ghee was made to Agni. The remainder of the ghee was then offered to Vishway devas. The priest took some water in one vessel. Using a flower, the priest sprinkled some of the consecrated water in all four directions and a few drops on the newly-weds. He applied holy ash to the couple's foreheads. The couple then stood and prayed to Agni for various blessings. The priest took some water in a beaker, put a gold ornament in it and, using a flower, sprinkled the couple with appropriate mantras.

The couple: We offer this ghee to Agni. We offer the remaining ghee to Vishway devas (all gods and goddesses).

After applying holy ash to the couple's forehead, the priest asked them to stand before the fire and offer prayers. Ramesh and Meena spoke the Mantra.

Prayer (Mantra – Aashwalayana Shrauta Sutra 111)

'O god Agni, you are Om incarnate, and you represent the vowel sound in all syllables. We bow to you for you complete the Yajna (fire sacrifice). We beg forgiveness for our omissions and for our excesses in ritual. Grant us, O Agni, the conveyor of oblations, faith, intellect, success, understanding, learning, wisdom, riches, strength, long life, power and good health.'

Sprinkling of the couple by the priest (Mantra – Aitareya Brahmana 8.3)

Priest: With the inspiration from god Savita, with the arms of Ashwins, with the hands of god Pushana, with the brightness of Agni, with the lustre of the sun, with the power of god Indra, I sprinkle you with this water mixed with gold, so that you may be blessed with strength, riches, success and food. May this action turn out to be a sprinkling with nectar. May there be peace, prosperity and contentment.

Bringing the ceremony to a close

Then Meena's parents took water in their right hands and allowed it to trickle into the copper tray in front of them. 'May the Supreme Lord be pleased by this marriage sacrament of our daughter performed here.'

14)   *Verses of blessings*

The priest drew two swastika figures on the floor about two feet apart, using rice grains. Ramesh stood facing west on one figure, with a few rice grains in his hand. A silk cloth decorated with the symbols Om and Swastika was held by two close friends of the families as a screen in front of Ramesh. Meena, with rice in her hand, escorted by her honorary maternal uncle, arrived and stood on the swastika opposite Ramesh, facing east. They could not see each other as they were separated by the silk cloth. Two girls stood behind the couple holding water vessels. Rice grains tinged with red kumkum were distributed among the guests. The priest and others sang eight or nine verses of blessing. Each verse ended with a refrain – '*Kuryat sada mangalam, shubha mangala saavadhaan*' (Hark! This is the auspicious moment bringing blessings to the couple). After each refrain the guests showered the newly-weds with their blessings in the form of a few rice grains.

After the verses, the screen was removed, and a little consecrated water was applied to the couple's eyes. Ramesh and Meena put rice grains on each other's heads. Then they garlanded each other, indicating their acceptance of each other. The guests applauded with enthusiasm and traditional music was played to celebrate the occasion.

Verses of blessings (traditional verses from the Purana text) Pandit Gopal read the translation before the singing to make the verses meaningful to all.

(1) I offer homage to the god Ganapati, who has a large belly, and who removes obstacles. This son of Shiva has a sharp tusk, a reddish complexion and is revered by other gods. May he bless you.

(2) May the holy rivers, Ganga, Sindhu, Sarasvati, Yamuna, Godavari, Narmada, Kaveri, Sharayu, Mahendra Tanaya, Charmanvati, Vedika, Kshipra, Vetravati, Gandaki and Purna, along with the oceans, bring you good fortune.

(3) May the 14 rare objects – jewels – churned up from the ocean – Lakshmi, Kaustubh, Parijataka, Liquer, Physician, the moon, wish-granting cow, Indra's elephant, Rambha the heavenly nymph, sun's horse, deadly poison, Vishnu's bow, conch shell and nectar, bless you every day.

(4) I offer homage to Brahman, the Supreme Spirit of Hinduism, who is praised by Brahma, Varuna, Indra Rudra and Maruts with heavenly hymns, whom the singers of Saman praise, whom the *yogins* perceive with their deep meditation and whose limits are unknown by gods and demons. May Brahman bless you always.

179

(5) May your status as married householders bring you good fortune. This Ashrama supports the other three Ashramas, namely, students, retired folk and renouncers. It has inspired kings like Janaka to do the public good. May this Ashrama bring you good luck always.

(6) May your new status bring you good fortune, children and good qualities to make everyone proud. Offer worship to and do the Will of God through selfless honest work.

(7) You are ending your student stage and becoming married householders. Be happy, have heroic children, succeed in this world, enhance the nation's prestige and live a hundred years.

(8) May Indra's good fortune obtained in the company of gods and praised by the ancient sages, bring you blessings and good luck.

(9) I offer silent worship to the divine feet of Vishnu, husband of Lakshmi, because that moment of remembrance is the essence of auspicious time and day, of the power of the planets and the moon, of wisdom and of providence.

15) *Blessings and good wishes of elders spoken in Sanskrit.*

(Mantra – Rig-Veda 10.85.46)

Jay:
'My daughter, be a queen with your husband's father, be a queen with your husband's mother, be a queen with your husband's sister, be a queen with your husband's brothers.'

The priest blesses the couple (Mantra – Rig-Veda 10.85.42)

'Remain and act as a couple without any differences of opinion. May you be blessed with a long life. May you happily live in your own home playing with your sons and grandsons.'

The priest blesses the couple (Mantra – Rig-Veda 10.191.4)

May your hearts hold similar intentions and thoughts. May you act with one mind. May your actions reflect unity of purpose.'

The priest blesses the guests (Mantra – Rig-Veda 10.161.4)

'May you progressively prosper and live to enjoy a hundred autumn, winter and spring seasons. Worship and propitiate the gods Indra, Agni, Savita and Brihaspati. Being pleased they will grant you a further hundred years.

'May there be peace, peace, peace.'

Meena and Ramesh together made *namaskar* to Pandit Gopal and gave his fee in cash, since theirs was a spiritual relationship, and not a business contract.

Many guests gave gifts or cash with their congratulations. Everyone enjoyed the feast lunch.

16) *Prayers to the seven sages and the Pole Star*

In the evening of the wedding day Pandit Gopal guided the couple as they offered prayers to the seven sages and Arundhati. Ramesh said: 'May my bride be like the constant Arundhati. May the Pole Star, who is always constant, bless us with constancy in our married life and protect us from our enemies.'

Prayers to Ursa Major (Mantra – Bauddhayana Grihya Sutra 1.5.14)

Ramesh: These are the seven sages who placed Arundhati, the foremost among the six stars in the Krittika asterism, alongside them in a firm position in the galaxy. The six Krittikas (Pleiades) bring great prosperity; may she (the bride) shine for us as the eighth.

Prayer to the Pole Star (Mantra – Hiranyakeshi Grihya Sutra 19.7.1)

Ramesh: O, Bright One, you are constant and firm. You engender constancy. You are constancy incarnate. You, through your firmness, hold other asterisms in place. You are the pivot at the centre of the circle of stars. Protect me from my enemies.

17) *The newly-weds enter their home*

Then Meena and Ramesh entered their home, after bowing before the elders in the family. Both placed their right foot on the threshold. A pot filled with grain was pushed by Meena with her foot so that the grain would scatter into the house. This would bring food, prosperity and good luck into the home. Ramesh said, 'I enter this house gladly with my bride. May she give me brave sons. I shall live in this house with my wife in complete happiness.' He then said to his wife, 'May you be happy in your new home. You are the mistress of the house. May we grow old together and praise our happy home to our friends.'

Entering their home (Mantra – Bauddhayana Grihya Sutra 1.5.7)

Ramesh: I enter this auspicious house (with my bride) with a happy heart. This house will not kill brave sons; it will be filled with their voices and presence. Here will flow food, water and ghee to nourish brave sons. Here I will live happily with my wife.

Ramesh (Mantra – Rig-Veda 10.85.27)

'My wife, may your liking (for your stay in your husband's home) increase with your future children. Be ever vigilant about your householder's duty as the mistress of this house. When we grow old together we shall sing praises of this house among our friends.'

18) *Laxmi Pujan (The bride's new name)*

The bride is Lakshmi, the goddess of good fortune incarnate. On her welfare depends the fortune and stability of her new family. She is offered welcome with new clothes, ornaments and sweet dishes. She has a new status and a new home. All connection with her natal family comes to an end. Her husband's family take the responsibility for her welfare. She is now given a new first name and welcomed as a new member of the family. Sometimes the natal first name is retained.

New first name of the bride

On this auspicious day I retain the first name of my wife. Ramesh said: May this name – Meena – be firmly established and approved.

Priest and guests

'May you have a long life and a happy married life. May you be blessed with daughters and sons as you wish. We wish you good luck.'

Meena and Ramesh, Ashok and Manjiri, Jay and Lata and the grandparents of the newly-weds offered prayers to the family deities for the successful completion of the marriage rituals.

The next day Meena and Ramesh travelled by train to Devon Hotel in Exeter for their honeymoon. They had caught an early train from Paddington station. Ashok, who was now a senior booking administrator for British Rail, had booked their return tickets at reduced rates, a facility which all staff enjoyed. The train journey did not last for more than three hours and the newly-weds arrived at Exeter station about noon. A short taxi ride brought them to the hotel, where a double room with en-suite facilities was booked and provided the privacy they needed. After signing the register Meena and Ramesh were shown to their room on the second floor by the hotel porter, who carried their suitcases. Ramesh tipped the porter and as he left the room, Meena closed the door and they rushed into each other's arms in the middle of the room. That free physical contact was thrilling and the kiss that followed expressed their full dormant physical desire. A full five minutes later they separated.

Meena said that she was going to unpack the suitcases and arrange their belongings in the wardrobe, the chest of drawers and the dressing table. Ramesh helped for a few minutes and then said that he was going to visit the nearby chemist for the necessary supplies. While Ramesh was out Meena completed the unpacking. Ramesh soon returned and put the small paper bags in the bedside cabinet. Then they went to the hotel dining room for lunch.

The head waiter showed them to their table and told them to sit at the same table for all their meals during their stay. As they sat at the secluded table near the window, they could see all the comings and goings near the entrance of the hotel. They enjoyed a glass of white wine with the main course of roast chicken and vegetables, and ordered sliced banana with vanilla ice-cream as the sweet.

While they were having coffee a motorcycle noise made them look out through the window. A strongly built young man and a very attractive young woman were still on the seats as the gleaming blue and white machine pulled up near the entrance. As they removed their helmets their pink skin and yellow hair became visible. The man had tanned forearms. The woman wore very tight slacks and a tight blue sweater which threw her plump hips and prominent, proud breasts sharply on view. Ramesh looked at the machine and the couple, and became silent.

Meena looked at the girl's breasts, which had been in close contact with the man's back as they had pulled up. When the girl turned to get down from the pillion seat, Meena noticed her stimulated nipples making two small bumps against the fabric of the blue sweater. That sight triggered off her deep memory bank and transported her mind to her distant past, beyond the death barrier, to the occasion when, she clearly recalled, she herself had pressed her budding breasts against the back of the man who was riding the motorcycle.

The motorcycle had triggered Ramesh's memory bank and his mind was transported back to his distant past, beyond the death barrier, where his mind's eye clearly saw a young man resembling himself and also saw the young woman on the pillion seat as the spitting image of Meena.

They both finished their coffee and, still in a trance, left the dining room hand in hand and made their way up to their room. Meena put the 'do not disturb' card on the door handle on the outside and closed and locked the door. The whole present world was shut out and their innermost spirits entered and guided their bodies to enact a past experience, completely oblivious of their present condition or location.

Now, in July 1975, they were alone together in a hotel room where their present bodies were guided to enact a 'once-in-a-lifetime' experience by their minds mesmerised by their past existence.

'Do you remember what I said on the day you got your degree result?' said Meena.

'Do remind me.'

'I said that I would be yours on our wedding night, but,' continued Meena, 'we can pretend that it is our wedding night although this is the afternoon of the day after our wedding day.'

'Yes, I'll go along with that,' said Ramesh.

'I think a warm shower would help us relax. What do you think, Ramesh?'

'A good idea... Let us shower to—'

'Why do you stop?'

'If I say the word it might shock you, Meena.'

'Say the word and see if I am shocked.'

'Shower together.'

'I am not shocked, darling, I am curious.'

'Meena, I suggested that because I think we should see each other without our clothes.'

'Why?'

'That will give you some idea of what you have to take into your body.'

'That will also enable you to see my secret opening,' said Meena. They removed their clothes slowly so that each could see the gradual disrobing of the other. They went into the bathroom and as Meena bent over the end of the bath to start the shower, Ramesh gently caressed her well-defined rump. When the showerhead produced a warm flow, both got into the bath and pulled the shower curtain to prevent the water from splashing on to the floor. Ramesh held the showerhead in his hand and 'bathed' Meena's body and Meena did the same to Ramesh. It was a thrilling experience, when they rubbed the other's body and felt the vital parts. When Ramesh was gently running his finger along Meena's secret opening, she held his pointer in her hand for the first time. The pointer grew bigger and hard. Ramesh quietly removed her questing hand and turned off the shower. They pulled back the shower curtain, got out of the bath and began to dry themselves on the soft towels.

When they went back to the bedroom, Meena put her towel on her head and, wrapping it round her long hair, wound it like a turban.

'I love you,' whispered Ramesh.

'I love you,' responded Meena.

Gradually they lowered themselves on to the bed. 'I'll not hurt you. I'll be gentle,' he said.

'I know ... but it is still going to hurt when you make me a woman.'

'I bought things this morning – let me show you.' He got up from the bed and took out the small paper bags from the bedside cabinet. 'Look, I have got some condoms and jelly to smooth the operation.'

Meena looked at the packets and the tube. 'When you have rubbed the jelly on my secret opening and put some inside as well, I'll put the "helmet" on your soldier and get him ready for the battle.'

Ramesh smeared the jelly on her maidenhair, her nether lips and put some into the opening. Meena fitted a condom and rolled it down to the base of his pointer. Then she lay on her back and opened her thighs.

'It is going to hurt this first time because I have to tear the curtain with my pointer.' He got in between her thighs and brought his pointer close to the entrance of her passage. Gently he pushed it into the opening until he felt the barrier. He whispered into her ear to be brave. Then he put his lips on her lips, lifted her bottom slightly and pushed very hard to break the curtain, and occupied the cave.

As Meena felt the tearing pain, she clung to him and said – *Raj, Raj, Raj.* At that moment he said – *Maya,*

Maya, Maya. Their mesmerised spirits had given voice to their past identity. Throughout the disrobing, the shower, and the first intimate body contact, Meena had felt no sense of shame. As a result of friction when Ramesh's pointer began to pour out his energy into the rubber bag, her sense of shame returned. When Ramesh withdrew from the battlefield, she quickly left the bed, covered herself with the towel and went into the bathroom. As she felt the pain she put her hand on to her opening and pressed the towel to deaden the ache. A few drops of blood trickled from the battle scar on to the towel. She sat on the loo to pass water then cleaned herself and put on some soothing cream on her opening and wrapping the towel round her middle, she went back to the bedroom and lay down on the mattress next to Ramesh. He put his arm round her and gently kissed her to soothe her ache.

'I am now a woman,' she whispered, and they both lay quietly on the bed and drifted off to sleep. Two hours later they felt a little refreshed when they awoke from their deep sleep. Ramesh felt thirsty. He got up, drank some water and made two cups of coffee for them. Meena was reminded of her new status as a woman by the dull ache. She winced as she slowly left the bed and went to the bathroom. After coffee she decided to have a warm bath to soothe her recently tattered feminine core.

Ramesh had recovered from his tiring experience and as he dressed, his pointer was raring to find the newly discovered heaven. When Meena came into the bedroom after her bath, Ramesh hugged her and pressed his hand into her groin.

'No, no don't. I am sore,' she said firmly.

After the evening meal, they returned to their room and retired early for the night.

188

Step Eight

Meena's married life proper began on the second day of her honeymoon. She had been apprehensive of the new role she was expected to play. She had read the theory of the physical act yet she had not been at all confident whether she would measure up to her husband's expectations. She was under a strange influence from the past, and she felt that Ramesh was also affected by the memory of the past. They had both enacted a past experience in a trance. Her husband had removed her innocence in a natural yet traumatic fashion. She had fought a bloody battle and the battle scar was a reminder of that event as she busied herself with her morning rituals, bathing and getting dressed to face her first day as a 'married woman'.

Ramesh had showered and dressed first and after she was ready, they went to the dining room for breakfast. As they sat at their allotted table, Ramesh picked up his cup and said, 'Good morning, wife.'

'Good morning, husband,' she responded likewise. They both looked at each other seriously and then simultaneously burst out laughing.

After breakfast, she wanted to sit in the hotel lounge and quietly read the newspaper or a magazine. But Ramesh was full of energy and insisted that they went out for a walk. She resisted his suggestion at first, but his persistence overcame her wishes and she had to follow his wishes.

'Am I going to be a meek and mild Hindu wife? I must

be careful not to subordinate my personality to my husband's wishes', she thought to herself but did not say anything.

After playing the masterful husband and making her bend to his wishes, Ramesh was very attentive and demonstrated his affection and love by putting his hand on her shoulder and also holding her hand as they walked leisurely in the city. Ramesh put his arm around her waist whenever they had to cross the road. As they came to a florist's shop, Ramesh went in and bought a single white rose for her. 'I love you, Meena,' he said.

'I love you, Ramesh,' she said.

He fleetingly kissed her on the mouth before continuing their ambling.

'I would like a cup of tea,' she said.

They went into a café, where she had tea and Ramesh wanted ice cream. It had been a pleasant walk. When they returned to the hotel and went up to their room, Ramesh embraced her wildly and kissed her passionately. She was still sore where it mattered and was not willing to take part in a vigorous love play. She hugged and kissed but stopped Ramesh from touching her between her thighs. For the time being Ramesh took the hint and released her from his embrace.

'I hope he leaves me alone for a day or two', she thought to herself. She noticed that there was a good film on television that afternoon and hoped to see it after lunch. But her husband had other plans. Ramesh had got his science degree in August 1973 and up to his marriage in July 1975 he had not managed to get a job, although he had tried very hard. His parents were quite well off and had continued to give their son a generous weekly allowance, but Ramesh had not found any hobby to occupy his mind. Now that he had married Meena, whom he loved, he lusted after the pleasure of the flesh between her thighs and his mind was gripped by the thought of Meena's soft and exciting body. Meena had firmly indicated that she was sore and therefore unwilling to experience any physical contact. He, on the other hand, was quietly planning to establish his right to her 'goodies' as her legally wedded husband. He did not speak his thoughts, yet that was what occupied his mind. He had read in a men's magazine that when a woman says 'no', she might mean it to be a 'maybe', or might even mean 'yes' if the man demonstrated his desire in a masterful and masculine way.

Ramesh was fully aware of the trauma Meena had suffered when he had removed her virginity only the previous afternoon. It was less than twenty-four hours ago. Her opening was wounded and sore. His head understood her unwillingness. But his heart and rising lust wanted to bury his stiffened resolve in her soothing heaven. For over an hour, after they had returned from their walk, there was a real battle going on between his head and his heart. He had not arrived at any course of action in his mind as they went to the dining room for lunch.

'Shall we have some wine?' he asked.

'I don't want any,' said Meena, 'but you have it if you want.'

'Come on, one glass won't hurt.'

'No, I don't want it,' she said firmly. He ordered a glass for himself, which he enjoyed with his lunch.

Meena noticed a certain gleam in her husband's eyes throughout lunch. She had no idea what he was thinking about. She put it down to the effect of the wine. But it was a mixture of the wine and uncontrollable lust. Ramesh was like a boy who was going to have his toy, and also he was a man who was determined to establish his control over his wife.

After lunch Ramesh persuaded Meena to return to their room, although she was hoping to see the afternoon film on television. He locked the door and taking Meena in his arms began to unbutton her summer frock. When she began to resist, he kissed her forcefully and succeeded in removing her dress. Then he backed her up to the bed. He pulled the cover with one hand while still kissing her and gradually they both fell on the bed. In the supine position he was able to continue kissing her and handling her breasts, gently at first, then quite firmly. He gave her no chance to say a word of protest since he pressed his mouth on hers and inserted his tongue in between her lips. Under this intense kissing, he unclipped her bra and pushed the cups over her breasts. Now he began to gently rub them with the palm of his right hand until he could feel her nipples becoming stiff. In between rubbing both breasts, he pinched her nipples between his thumb and forefinger. Meena's lips were becoming a little sore, yet the concentrated attention paid to her lips, breasts and nipples was gradually softening her resistance. She began to make whimpering noises.

Ramesh stealthily pressed his fingers over her mound, then under her pants and on to her maidenhair and the nether lips. His questing fingers became damp with her lubrication. Meena's mind, through fear of pain, was reluctant to take part in the physical act, yet her glands had reacted to stimulation and her opening was being lubricated.

Be that as it may, Ramesh had some difficulty with his pointer, which was over-lubricated. Before he could do anything, he had to remove his trousers and underpants, fit a condom on his overheated pointer and hope to find its heaven. Meena lay still for a few minutes. Ramesh took a chance. He undressed, put on a condom and was about to remove Meena's knickers when he lost control and his energy spurted out into the rubber bag. He was very disappointed that he could not insert the pointer into its rightful haven. He had promised so much through his manful actions but could not deliver the packet. Meena's body was ready to admit the intruder but her opening remained empty. Ramesh left the bed and went into the bathroom to dispose of the condom and clean himself. He was quite shamefaced when he came back to bed and lay down in silence.

Meena went into the bathroom, sat on the loo and gently rubbed her clit to remove the ache caused by the unfulfilled promise. There was no climax only a little comfort. Back she came to the bedroom. When she lay on the bed next to Ramesh, he whispered to her that he was sorry.

'You kept me waiting too long,' he said, blaming her for his shortcoming.

'I told you that I was sore, but you refused to understand. Never mind, darling. Tomorrow we'll make it.'

Ramesh drank two glasses of wine in the evening to mask his failure.

Next day Ramesh and Meena did not attempt any physical intimacy. That bit of rest had diminished the soreness of Meena's portal. She had a long hot bath after breakfast and used soothing cream to bring her a little comfort. Surprisingly, Meena felt very tender towards her husband because he did not try to force her to follow his will. But Ramesh's head was full of lustful longings. Two days later, when Meena was willing, Ramesh was too eager and as a result lost control before Meena was ready. For her there was disappointment since the 'bloated' feeling didn't last for more than two minutes.

Ramesh acted with feverish enthusiasm which always resulted in a premature spilling for him, and there was no orgasm for Meena throughout the rest of the honeymoon; both of them experienced failure. Meena was eager to experience that feeling of ecstasy after an orgasm but her over-excitable husband could not help. The day they were due to return, when Ramesh was in the hotel lounge in the afternoon, Meena rubbed her opening and the sleeping clit with the lubricating jelly for many minutes until her passage throbbed and contracted round her index finger. At least she had managed to have one finger-induced climax on her honeymoon.

When they returned to London, there was a letter waiting for Ramesh. He had sent an application to a firm of educational publishers, and he was asked to attend an interview in three days' time.

'I didn't know you were interested in a publishing job.'

'I'm not. This job has nothing to do with editing or book promotion, I sent an application for a job as a publisher's representative.'

'What would you have to do?' asked Meena.

'I don't know – but I'll tell you all about it after the interview. That is, if I get the job.'

On the morning of the interview, Ramesh took some pains to dress smartly. He wore a blue shirt with a maroon tie and put on his summer jacket with grey trousers. His shoes were well polished and his hair well combed. He made sure that he had his 'O' level, 'A' level and degree certificates with him.

When he arrived at the London Books office, he was shown to the waiting room, where there were two men and a woman who had also come for their interviews. The woman and one of the men had their interviews before Ramesh.

'Good morning, Mr Joshi. Take a seat. I am John Thompson. I'm in charge of sales.'

'I have read the leaflet giving details of the schoolbooks published by your company. What age group are these books designed for?' asked Ramesh.

'Our books are written for secondary school pupils, from thirteen years old. Some are for 'O' level pupils,

194

that is fifteen- and sixteen-year-olds, and some are for 'A' level pupils,' Mr Thompson explained.

'What would my job involve?'

'You will work as our School Rep, so you will visit different schools, meet the science and maths teachers and try to sell the books to the school. The schools usually buy sets of thirty copies.' John Thompson was an energetic man in his late thirties. He examined Ramesh's educational documents and gave more information. 'Are you looking for a permanent job, Mr Joshi?'

'Yes, I think the job has challenges and it will be full of variety. I don't have a car but I am hoping to learn to drive and get a car eventually.'

'A car could help but it is not essential. Your salary will be about £900 a year. You will get your travelling expenses, and where you have to stay overnight, the firm will arrange your hotel accommodation. Are you interested in the job?'

'Yes certainly,' replied Ramesh.

'I notice you are Ramesh Ashok Joshi. Why do you call yourself Ramesh and not Ashok?'

'My parents originate from western India where the system of personal names is different from other areas of the Subcontinent. I am Ramesh, my second name is in fact my father's first name. Joshi is the family name, so I will answer to Ramesh and not to Ashok.'

Ramesh was asked to remain in the waiting room for half an hour or so while the fourth candidate was interviewed.

An hour later, all four candidates were called back to John Thompson's office. There was a smart young woman sitting by Mr Thompson. 'Well, lady and gentlemen, you all have been successful.'

Peter Martin, Alan Smith and Joyce Chancellor were the other candidates.

'The firm has decided to expand its operation. We are

appointing Ramesh Joshi and Peter Martin as our Maths and Science reps and Alan Smith and Ms Joyce Chancellor will be our Arts and Humanities reps. This is Kitty Willow, our Reps Co-ordinator.

'Hello!' said Kitty Willow. 'I shall make your visit and travel arrangements. I have some leaflets here which need no further explanation. You will find your catchment area written there. You will have to visit many secondary schools in your area. I shall phone the schools and find out the suitable days and times. You will be able to get that information on Fridays. You will work in the office on Fridays, preparing your visits reports – you will be out in the field for four days. Contact me when you are in the field or see me here on Fridays. You will soon get the hang of it.'

'Thank you all. You all start next Monday, when you will get details about your pay and allowances. Good luck.' Mr Thompson bid them goodbye.

Ramesh was very happy to have got the job. He phoned his father and gave him the good news. He had a sandwich lunch and coffee and went back home and waited for Meena to return from her job as a trainee pharmacist.

When Meena came home Ramesh gave her all the details about the interview, the other successful candidates and the nature of his job. He mentioned the names of the Sales Director and the Reps Co-ordinator.

'Congratulations, darling,' said Meena, and kissed him with affection.

Ashok and Manjiri were very happy and proud of Ramesh and Meena. Ashok had a bottle of wine, which he opened before the evening meal, and they drank a toast to wish Ramesh and Meena success in their careers.

'Baba and Bai would have been very happy to learn that Ramesh has got a job,' said Ashok. 'I'll write and give them the good news. It was a pity that they had to go back to India only a couple of days after the wedding.'

That night Ramesh and Meena had to be very quiet when they wanted to have sex. Ramesh was very happy at getting the job and the glass of wine at dinner made him happier still. He became overexcited and hardly managed to put on a condom before he was pressing his lust into his unprepared wife. Meena was not ready when Ramesh poured out his lust mixed with love into the protective. Meena had yet another 'high and dry' experience. When Ramesh came back to bed after cleaning himself up, Meena was trying desperately to hold back her tears. When Ramesh put out the light, Meena's tears flowed silently and made her pillow damp She turned her pillow over, then turned on to her side facing away from her husband and allowed sleep to soothe her aching heart.

Ramesh began to criticise Meena's actions, and almost every day tried to impose his likes and dislikes on her. It caused her a great deal of distress. Manjiri noticed that Meena was becoming very quiet and suffering in silence after listening to Ramesh's unreasonable comments. Meena was enjoying her job as a trainee pharmacist and wished that her husband would encourage her, support her and appreciate her progress. Ramesh was beginning to behave like a resentful child if he didn't have his own way. It all started because of his failure to enjoy sex with Meena. Meena tried to tell him that he should read a good sex manual and learn to control his ejaculation until she was well-oiled and ready to experience a climax in his embrace. He attempted to improve his technique but his brain was overactive with lustful thoughts, which caused his premature spilling and ended in disappointment for them both.

At least he was learning to be a good rep for his company. Things continued in this manner for six months or more.

* * *

It was spring time in 1976. The weather was turning warm. One day when they had their lunch on a Saturday, Meena broached the subject of finding a flat where she and Ramesh could live and take responsibility for their daily lives, manage their budget and take decisions for themselves. She waited for some reaction from Ashok, Manjiri or Ramesh. Manjiri appeared to hesitate and made no comment. Ashok kept quiet to see what Ramesh would say. Ramesh broke the awkward silence.

'We are quite happy here. We have our room. Mum and Dad are here to take care of things. We don't need to find a flat. I like to live here.'

'But I think we should try to be independent and run our lives in the way we want. We are in Britain and not in India. We need to form a nuclear family unit ourselves and not continue the "joint family" concept. I want us to get a flat where I can run the show and be in charge.' Meena expressed herself quite reasonably and forcefully. But alas, Ramesh was very reluctant to leave his parents.

'Look, Meena,' he said, 'I am now getting the hang of my job and in the near future I may be staying away overnight for two days a week at least. Surely you don't want to be alone in a flat? You will have Mum for company and you will be safe here.'

'Don't you want to enjoy privacy with your wife? Do things together? Do mundane everyday things like shopping, cleaning the flat, cooking, doing the washing up? That way we can form a close unit and not depend on your parents. They will be there to help and guide if we run into any difficulty, but we need to try and live independently in order to face life together.'

'I like the idea of a joint family. I like living with my

parents. You are a member of this family and I think you will be very happy here.'

'Ramesh, I am not suggesting that your mum is behaving like the proverbial Indian mother-in-law. I am well looked after here. But I want us to live independently.'

'I like it here and you should respect your husband's wishes,' said Ramesh.

The argument stopped there but it did not end. Meena realised that she had been dominated yet once more, and she did not like the future prospect.

Time went on in a repressed manner. Weeks rolled into months, then years. She tried her best to wean Ramesh from the protective and smothering wings of his mother. Two years later she was still living with Ramesh's parents and she was experiencing bad, unfulfilled sex.

It was at the office Christmas party in 1977, that an opportunity came Ramesh's way and it changed his life. Although there were other young women working in the office, Ramesh and other company reps had to deal with Kitty Willow every week. After being married for over two years and not finding any satisfying solution to his problem, Ramesh had thought that a woman from a different cultural background would perhaps be more suitable as a bosom friend. He had felt attracted to Kitty Willow for over six months. She was a confident and adventurous young woman who made friends easily and was not backward in coming forward to speak her mind freely and frankly.

'Hello, Ramesh. Are you having a good time?'

'Yes, Miss Willow.'

'Come on, drop the "Miss Willow" and call me Kitty. We've known and worked with each other for over two years.'

'Yes, and I have admired you from a distance from the first time I saw you.'

'You can admire me from close quarters.'

'Can we go out for a drink one Friday after work? There is so much I want to say.'

'Yes, why not,' responded Kitty. 'How about the Friday after the middle of January in the new year?'

'That would be perfect,' said Ramesh.

Over the Christmas break the Joshi and Bapat families met twice for the evening meal. All six of them enjoyed white wine with their chicken curry and other delicacies. Ramesh and Meena kept their innermost feelings and thoughts to themselves and did their best to paper over the cracks in their marriage. They exchanged presents. For once, Ramesh did not criticise the gift he received from Meena. It was a very expensive blue shirt, which he accepted with obvious pleasure. Meena received her favourite French perfume from her husband. But the friendly atmosphere dissolved early in the new year. Ramesh was eager to see Kitty.

They met at a wine bar near their place of work.

'Here's to you.' Kitty raised her glass.

'Here's to us,' said Ramesh.

Ramesh spoke about his marriage and his particular problem. Kitty told him about her mother and sister.

'I find you very desirable,' he said.

'I Iike you too, Ramesh. But you need some therapy for your problem.'

'I can't afford it.'

'Well, I can provide it and it would not cost you anything, not even the price of a meal, because we shall go Dutch. Is that a bargain?'

'Yes, it sounds promising,' he said.

'Ramesh, I live on my own in a flat of my own in west London. My sister looks after my mother and they live in the family house in Kentish Town. My father was a brute of a man. He walked out on us when I was at university. He was a domineering bully and always drank to excess. After university I got the job in the company, where I hope to stay for many years.'

'Shall we have another glass of wine?'

'No, not here. Look, why don't we go to my flat? We can have a sandwich with our wine. I'll give you your first therapy session.'

Ramesh and Kitty travelled by the Central line on the underground and reached Kitty's flat in about forty minutes.

'Relax, Ramesh. Warm yourself up near the fire while I prepare our sandwiches.'

Ramesh removed his overcoat, scarf and gloves and stood with his back to the gas fire and admired the tastefully decorated and neatly kept sitting room in Kitty's flat. In a few minutes Kitty brought a tray of sandwiches a bottle of wine and two glasses into the sitting room and put it on the coffee table. They ate the sandwiches and sipped the wine while Kitty explained her life's philosophy.

'After my bitter experience with my father, I made a vow to myself. I will not allow any man to dominate me, to influence my head or my heart. I am hard as nails above the navel but below the button I am soft and furry.'

Ramesh listened, rather confused.

'But,' continued Kitty, 'I like men for their velvety weapons, which are much better than the lifeless plastic ones. So, dear boy, let us begin your therapy. Come into the bedroom. We shall strip and see if I can begin to cure your problem.'

Without much delay they undressed. Kitty took out a small box and a tube from the bedside cabinet and went into the bathroom. She came back soon and showed him the small box.

'I told you that we'll go Dutch, didn't I? Well, I'm ready and the cap fits. In your first session you are to feast your eyes on my goodies. Kiss me, fondle me, touch me, even suck my points – but no connection. That way your senses will be desensitised and you will be able to control yourself. Today you will probably spill the beans in three minutes, but over the next three weeks you will achieve control for a longer time. Then you can dominate the pussy willow with your weapon. This evening you can feel the soft and furry pussy willow. You can feel free and enjoy your session. The sooner you are cured, the sooner you can dominate my pussy willow.'

It was a feast, visual and tactile, which had his lust reeling. Kitty also filled his ears with her explicit instructions and her appreciation of his efforts. She held his right hand over her nether lips and held his weapon over her navel. 'This is what I call my navel engagement.' In four minutes both experienced the relief from tension. Kitty kissed Ramesh on the lips and confirmed their sessions for the next three weeks.

Ramesh said that he had had to work late on his reports. His parents and Meena had no reason to doubt his explanation, and he relished his evening meal in a relaxed state of mind.

Over the following three Fridays, Kitty continued to provide therapy with much enthusiasm, and gradually Ramesh learned to keep his stiffened resolve under control, until during the third session he was able to withstand Kitty's verbal persuasions for nearly twenty minutes.

'Well done, good pupil,' she said, looking at the clock on the dressing table. 'Next week I shall reward your efforts.'

As planned, he did get his reward. His pointer plumbed the depths of Kitty's haven with much churning activity which had her rolling in her lather and planting kisses of gratitude on his mouth, neck, shoulders and chest. Then she spoke of her promise for the future. 'Ramesh, you

202

have satisfied Kitty Willow and conquered pussy willow, and both will be at your service as long as we continue to remain friends.'

That was the start of Ramesh's friendship with Kitty. He never gave a hint of it in the office. He worked hard at his job. He did not criticise Meena so often and rarely attempted to have sex with her.

Throughout 1978 Ramesh continued to dominate pussy willow. In October he had a very protected but rough session with Meena and at last provided her first orgasm in their three-year marriage.

Meena thought that Ramesh had thrown her a lifeline. She felt quite happy for some time but she still wanted to get a flat of their own. The opportunity to raise that subject did not come. Instead, Ramesh asked her to go with him to his company's office party at Christmas.

There she was introduced to Ramesh's colleagues. She met Kitty Willow, who had heard of Meena but not met her. Kitty spoke glowingly of Ramesh's work and efficiency. Meena sensed a little proprietorial tinge to Kitty's voice when she spoke of Ramesh. When she moved away with a glass of wine in her hand, Meena observed Kitty's 'friendly' attitude to the men she worked with and also noticed her prominent physical attributes. Meena had noticed something else. She had breathed in Kitty's body perfume and immediately made the connection. She had inhaled the same perfume on Ramesh's vest and shirts. For months she was puzzled but suddenly she got her positive clue. Ramesh and Kitty Willow were more than just colleagues. Over the Christmas break she went to see her mother and expressed her suspicions to her. She spoke of many incidents which surprised Lata. Jay and Lata had assumed that Meena was happily married to Ramesh.

Their assumption was shattered when Meena told them that she was going to confront Ramesh and his parents during the Christmas break.

On Boxing Day, Meena had her verbal boxing match with Ramesh in the presence of Ashok and Manjiri. 'I am going to leave you, Ramesh.' That was a bombshell for Ramesh's parents coming from the young daughter-in-law. They were stunned.

'Why? Tell us,' they said.

Meena spoke in a disappointed tone of voice. She had fallen in love with Ramesh and thought that Ramesh loved her too. Then she mentioned his domineering attitude towards her. And she mentioned the 'body perfume'.

'I thought Ramesh was faithful to me, but he has been having an affair with a woman in his office. Let him deny it.'

Ashok and Manjiri asked Ramesh whether it was true.

'Yes, it is true,' confessed Ramesh.

'That has killed our marriage,' she said. 'There was a connection between us from our past lives, when he was Raj and I was Maya. We were married but our marriage and our lives ended in an accident. In that relationship death and separation were brought by a motorcycle. In this life, in this relationship, an "office bicycle" has intervened and made me determined to seek a divorce. I shall leave this house tomorrow and start divorce proceedings in due course. I walked the "seven steps" with Ramesh in the hope that the union was for life. I was wrong. I am going to take the eighth step out of a bad marriage and live independently. I have the courage to rectify my error.'

The very next day Meena did take the eighth step, hoping to rebuild her shattered life. She looked forward to an independent and self-confident tomorrow. The eighth step would take her towards a promising dawn.